BEYOND REALITIES
2015

ANTHOLOGY
OF THE LUNA PRESS PUBLISHING
"WRITERS & ILLUSTRATORS CONTEST"

VOL I

EDITED BY ROBERT S MALAN

First published 2015 by Luna Press Publishing

Cover by Simon Walpole © 2015
2015 © of each story is with individual author
Editorial © Robert S Malan 2015

First published by Luna Press Publishing 2015

WWW.LUNAPRESSPUBLISHING.COM

ISBN-13: 978-1-911143-00-0

CONTENTS

To enter the Luna Press Publishing "Writers and Illustrators Contest" and for more great original works visit www.lunapresspublishing .com.

FOREWORD

Luna Press Publishing came back to life on January 1st 2015, after a long gestation period. It was my intention to nurture the seed of a dream and make it grow.

Luna has always been about opportunities - for me as both a writer and publisher; for a small team of new editors led by the superb Senior Editor Robert S Malan, and for the many writers and artists out there, all eager to embark on the next exciting project.

Beyond Realities, the Writers and Illustrators Contest, was created to introduce Luna to authors and artists of SF, Fantasy and Dark Fantasy, and in turn, to usher them into the path of a wider audience.

Needless to say we were petrified that no one would write in! As it turned out, we couldn't have been more wrong.

From January to September, we read an incredible amount of stories, and viewed some fine new art works. Originality, technical skills, innovation, understanding of the short story structure - these were some of the most important criteria we used to guide us through the selection process.

And so it is, with immense pride, that I introduce you to twelve captivating writers and one talented illustrator for the inaugural Writers and Illustrators Contest.

Sit down, relax, and let your journey, *beyond reality*, begin.

Thank you,
Francesca T. Barbini

NOTE:
THE ANTHOLOGY IS DIVIDED INTO THE THREE
GENRES OF THE CONTEST:
SCIENCE FICTION, FANTASY & DARK FANTASY.
WITHIN EACH SECTION, THE STORIES ARE
PRESENTED IN ALPHABETICAL ORDER BASED
ON AUTHOR'S SURNAME.

Science fiction

THE SWEDENBORG ANGLE

BY MONTAGUE CHAMBERS

'Emmanuel Swedenborg,' said my friend. 'Have you heard of him?'

The university, following the Great War, was a good place to be. It offered a secure, comfortable environment, away from the economic uncertainty of the world outside. Goodall College was modern enough to allow for a range of research in disciplines such as Physics, Engineering and Applied Science. It was also, paradoxically, traditional, having been a foundation by a former Bishop. Religion therefore still played its part; the college was permeated by a gentle Anglicanism and many Fellows attended the evening chapel. Even so, Kanton's question caught me off guard.

I could only stare blankly. I was sure that I had come across the name somewhere but could not place it. Kanton harrumphed.

'Emmanuel Swedenborg,' he began didactically, 'born January 1688, the year of the "Glorious Revolution", and died 1772. Started off as a scientist and an engineer; ended as a theologian and a mystic. Interesting man. Actually came from a mining family and got his first big break when he was appointed the Assessor of Mines by Charles XII of Sweden.

'That started him off and he began producing scientific work and descriptions of inventions and discoveries.' He looked at me, his eyes brilliant with the fervour of a missionary. 'He even sketched a design for a flying machine, years before the Wright brothers. He also suggested the functions of the neuron when people weren't even studying the brain. He was years ahead of his time but not arrogant about it.'

Unlike some, I thought to myself - but wisely didn't say this aloud - Kanton had a great opinion of himself. It was unwise to challenge this, although admittedly he was brilliant in some areas of study.

'He was offered the Chair of Mathematics at Uppsala but turned it down, preferring to study Chemistry, Metallurgy and Geometry.' He gave this last subject an odd emphasis and, noticing my raised eyebrows, nodded in satisfaction, as if he was privy to a great secret. 'Oh yes, that last bit is vital and crucial to everything.' He took a drink and continued, while fiddling with a gyroscope on the desk.

'From the 1730s he became increasingly interested in spiritual matters and determined to examine them with the same earnestness he had brought to his scientific studies. In his later life, he began having strange dreams and visions.' He snorted. 'Nowadays they would say he was having a breakdown and lock him up before he had any great insights into anything. Our moribund society.'

I waited patiently. It was best not to interrupt or hurry Kanton when he was in full flow.

'Then, in 1747, he resigned from his ordinary work and began writing books about his visits to the spiritual world, which he claimed he could visit at will. He talked about the world of angels and spirits and how he communicated with them all, including Jesus Christ and the Virgin Mary.

'At first it seemed a lot of rambling nonsense from a man who was perhaps the last great natural philosopher of the Renaissance. His thoughts and ideas constantly swapped and changed. One day he would be writing a volume on physiology or surgery and the next day trying to invent a better clock. Then of course there was all the mystical writing about Heaven and the angels. At first, one was inclined to treat it as the ramblings of a loony. There is a core of genius however, when you see past the shallow surface.'

He glared at me as if defying me to object or offer a counter argument. I merely nodded assent however. He harrumphed again and continued.

'I began to get into his work on crystallography. He is really seen as the father of that science; of categorising and separating out the crystal forms, using geometric shapes like pyramids, rhomboids and dodecahedrons.'

He tapped the book in front of him, which I supposed was one of Swedenborg's works. His eyes had the light of a fanatic.

'When you put the work on Geometry together with the work on crystals, it all begins to take form.'

He seemed unconscious of the slight pun he had just made and began waving his hands in the air with large expansive gestures.

'Later people called him a mystic, which is the term they use for someone they're too polite to call mad, outright. But he wasn't mad. He predicted the date of his own death and, on his death bed, he was offered the opportunity to recant by his pastor. The pastor, Ferelius, thought that Swedenborg had written all that stuff about spirits just to make himself famous.

'Swedenborg reportedly put his hand on his heart and said that everything he had written was true and there was even more that he could have said, if he had been allowed.' He looked at me triumphantly. 'There! You see? That is the new work I am undertaking. I want to understand Swedenborg's system. Somewhere in it must be the key to the other world; the answer to how he was able to visit the spirit world at will.'

'You believe it's a real place,' I murmured, frowning, and he sneered at me.

'Swedenborg was a scientist. He said this stuff was real. If he went there, it's a real place, whether in this dimension or another. If he could get there, so can others.'

'You think he left the key to the process in his work,' I said, enlightenment dawning.

'Exactly!' he said with satisfaction. 'And I mean to prove it.'

That was the start of it and he was certainly earnest in his endeavour. For months I hardly saw him or, if I did see him at the university, he would wave me away imperiously when I tried to speak. The Faculty asked me about him and I could only say that he was working on a truly novel work for which they would have to wait. Although he was a funded Research fellow, they were surprisingly patient and he was left in peace.

Despite his being fairly closed about his work, news of it inevitably travelled to the Reverend Arthur, Dr Reynolds, who was both the College chaplain and on the Board of Governors. I had found him a genial, urbane kind of parson and I was surprised when he mentioned Kanton's work to me and said that he had talked to him about it at length.

That last, I could believe; Kanton loved an audience when he was in the right mood. He would have jumped at the chance to pontificate at Dr Reynolds especially, as he could spout all that Swedenborg stuff and make out that he knew more about spiritual matters than a man of God.

In March, we were both called to see him. He was flushed and excited.

'I have read a work by Marconi, the father of radio,' he began almost as soon as we were through the door. 'He tried to describe creating a machine for communicating with the world of the dead. You know, he was quite into this stuff and sat in on seances with Arthur Conan Doyle and Sir Oliver Lodge, the physicist.'

He looked at us as though expecting a reaction.

'Marconi's involvement,' he said, 'is apt, for the work that

I am involved in is the meeting point of religion and science. Swedenborg suggested the possibility and I, Kanton, will fulfill it.' He shuffled the papers in front of him and waved them about. 'The device - for there will be a device - will be put together using Swedenborg's ideas of Geometry, Crystallography and Engineering.' He chuckled. 'With, of course, a little help from the theories of Marconi and Nicolai Tesla, that brilliant Hungarian scientist who understood so much about the strange byways of energy and how to use them.

'Science will provide the access to that other place and religion the descriptive language and guide as to what I shall find there. Too long has religion cowered fearfully in the shadows. Now is the time to claim her birthright. Science and religion, hand in hand, assaulting Heaven!'

Dr Reynolds, who had remained remarkably calm and silent throughout this speech, found this statement not so much blasphemous, as deeply conceited and even a little frivolous. He said so.

Kanton took no notice of him and his brow furrowed in thought. 'My problem is that of being an explorer to an unknown region,' he observed. 'The travellers' tales I have are too few and mostly fanciful. They are too coloured by the religious expectation of the visitor.' He nodded to both of us. 'Even Swedenborg wasn't immune from that problem,' he said ruefully. He pursed his lips and drummed his fingers on the desk. A strange faraway look came into his eyes. 'What I need,' he said thoughtfully, 'is some first hand experience of that other world. Direct observation, such as a brief sortie, to spy out the way.'

We stared at him.

'Well, that's impossible,' objected Reynolds, breaking in, 'unless you happen to die and then, of course you'd get all the direct experience you want!' He smiled patronisingly. 'Of course you couldn't come back and tell anyone.'

'There are those who have come back,' answered Kanton carelessly.

Dr Reynolds frowned. 'Yes, but they were people who died during surgery and were brought back; or unfortunate suicides who were revived; unless you mean Spiritualism and I earnestly hope you do not.'

Kanton's eyes more than flickered. 'Exactly!' he said triumphantly. 'Suicides who were brought back!'

Dr Reynolds loked at him, horrified. 'You can't mean to ...' he said weakly. 'It's a sin. That would be ...' He searched for the right word but could find nothing stronger than, "immoral."

'Risky, more like!' I muttered, and Kanton looked at me appreciatively.

'I knew you'd see it,' he said.

'I said it was risky,' I pointed out, 'meaning I understand what you intend to try and the variables involved ... well, some of them perhaps, but that doesn't mean I approve.'

Kanton promptly launched into a declamatory speech about great advances in knowledge requiring great risks and I could tell that he had rehearsed it for just such an occasion as this. Dr Reynolds and I argued, protested, cajoled, tried to persuade him otherwise, and in the end made no impact upon him at all. I could see that he was quite resolved to make the attempt.

How serious Kanton was about his assault on the spiritual world, I didn't realise until some days later. I was working in the garden, weeding and thinning out the borders. I was interrupted by a shout from Helga, my German housekeeper.

'Please,' she blurted out breathlessly when she reached me, 'Herr Doctor, you are wanted. There is trouble with that man; at the crazy man's place.' She waved vaguely towards the town.

Helga's English had never been top standard but her cooking was seriously wonderful. She always referred to

Kanton as "that man" or "the crazy one," so I knew at once who she meant.

I put on my coat and hurried round to Kanton's flat, a set of shabby rooms, in an old university building, once a grand Science hall and now a neglected corner, where difficult Faculty members were accommodated. Here I found his daily cleaner in some distress; she had phoned Helga, being at a loss what to do, although I gathered she had also called an ambulance.

'Upstairs,' she pointed. 'He's upstairs.'

I didn't wait to hear any more and took the stairs two and three at a time, until I arrived at the small crowded room that Kanton used as a study. He was lying on the floor, his face blotchy. On the desk was half of a solution and, next to it, a hypodermic needle with some of the solution still visible in it. I looked from these back to the prone figure on the floor.

He nodded to me. 'Couldn't wait. I'll see for myself now. This has to work.' His eyes bulged and foam seeped out the corner of his mouth. 'Don't try and stop me,' he groaned. 'Don't you see, I have to go as far as I can? I have to know what the other world looks like, so I can refine my work to take account of its physical ...'

His voice trailed off and his face assumed a deep purple colour as he began making choking noises. There was no doubt he was having some kind of heart attack. Where was the ambulance?

In a burst of good timing, it arrived outside and Kanton was bundled into it. I joined him for the journey to the hospital, explaining to the ambulancemen that there were no relatives and I supposed that I was the closest thing he had to a friend.

On the way he went into arrest and one of the ambulancemen immediately commenced resuscitation on him. He seemed to recover but, as they went into the hospital, I heard someone call out, "He's arrested again!" and they rushed him off. After some time, a doctor emerged and explained that they had managed to resuscitate him once more and he was now resting, "as comfortably as could be expected".

As soon as it was allowed, I went in to see him and he glared at me reproachfully. 'Why did they bring me back so soon?' he demanded. 'Didn't you explain what I was trying to do?'

'Well ... er ... I ...' I spluttered helplessly.

His face took on a kind of evangelical enthusiasm. 'I was there, Peter. I saw it all: the rivers, the fields, streets and minarets, exactly as described in some of the spirit communications. The city of crystal towers, beside a golden sea of light. And they were there, the angels and spirits.' A strange look between wonder and revulsion took his face and he continued. 'They were not as one might have expected from religious descriptions; not at all, but they knew me; knew what I was trying to do. I have to try again.'

I argued with him until the nurse came and shooed me out. Then I had to face Dr Maggs, who was concerned about Kanton's state of mind, as well he might be. I had a long discussion with Maggs about committal.

'I don't think he is going to be of harm to others,' I urged the doctor. 'It's more whether he is of harm to himself. He can be persuaded, I'm sure. He just needs monitoring.'

Maggs relented and agreed to my setting him up in my home, where I could keep an eye on him. Dr. Reynolds also visited on a regular basis, but this had little effect on Kanton's passion. The room I had allocated him as a study was soon cluttered with piles of paper; the central desk covered in books of all shapes and sizes: paperbacks, hardbacks, textbooks and leather bound. At the top of the desk a small, black, leather bound book balanced precariously, pinned open at its central point.

Almost every night we argued. Disagreements about Swedenborg, crystallography, Marconi and radio, and the carrier wave. At this point, Kanton lost me completely by bringing in Advanced Pure Mathematics, hyperbolic geometry and concepts such as triangles with more than 180 degrees in the angles. He also began to wax lyrical over Quantum Theory, something I had never really grasped.

'Swedenborg understood that the answer was in the angles he had worked out for the crystal forms of the world,' he explained to me. 'As every crystal has its three dimensional form, created by specific angles and geometrical shapes, so with man. As man exists in the physical world but has his extension into the spiritual world - his spiritual self made of spiritual substance - so it follows that every crystal, with its geometrical form in the physical world, must have an extra dimension; an extension into the spiritual world; an angle that is not seen.

'Swedenborg understood this but did not have the language to describe it properly. But his work argues that the two fit together. If you can calculate the angle of difference between the physical world for an object and the spiritual dimension, you find the point at which they meet. At that point, it is possible to create a door and pass through it, using the carrier wave as an aid.'

I talked all this over with Dr. Reynolds. 'Is he crazy?' I asked, and Reynolds at once understood that I was again considering committal.

He gave a perfect vicar's reply. 'While what he says sounds logically scientific,' he said mildly, 'it is, in terms of spiritual science, not possible. To quote St. Paul, "for this body must put on incorruption." That is to say, that the body physical is replaced by the body spiritual. Therefore, one cannot simply step through a door into the world of death because one is encumbered by the material form. Only as spiritual form can we enter into that other state.'

I put this to Kanton at our next meeting.

'Dr. Reynolds isn't stupid, is he?' he smiled. 'But that is where Quantum Theory comes in. If I can generate a field at the subatomic level, of the right frequency, I believe that it will divest my physical form of the material, leaving only the spiritual substance behind. And, as that spiritual substance, I can step through the door.'

There was no real answer to this, as it sounded like gibberish anyway. Kanton, however, descended into frantic work. I tried discussing with him how we might integrate him back into the Faculty, but he dismissed the university with a scornful laugh. The walls of the study became covered with diagrams and equations. One side, to the left of the desk, became fully occupied by a large panel with many switches, dials and levers. Its central area contained a hollow circle with a magnificent quartz crystal precariously suspended in its centre, the apex of the crystal aiming towards a point in front of the desk.

Finally Dr Reynolds and I were called or, rather, summoned. When we entered the office, Emmanuel was sitting at the desk. He looked up and gave a curious smile. 'Everything is ready,' he said. 'I have found it. I have found Swedenborg's angle of difference. I know how to make the door. All I have to do is step through it.'

I began stammering, along the lines of, 'It can't be real. How much of this is schizophrenia talking and how much is real? Have you really stumbled on to something that no one has seen before?'

He made me promise: 'When all this is achieved and I am gone, you must catalogue my work. You must gather it all up so that it can be examined by other scientists, so that they can understand what I have done and where I have gone. It may be that once there, I cannot come back, or I may not want to come back. Someone must take the next step and calculate the means of return. Then there will be coming and going as of old, and we will truly bring Heaven down to Earth!'

A protest rose on Dr Reynolds' lips and died.

Kanton started to flip a series of serpent switches and dials. A low humming began. I looked at him, thinking, 'This is really happening; he really thinks he's doing it.' The humming was on a particular note, like the low droning of a large bumble bee and I started feeling very strange and disassociated, like I was drunk.

He stood up and walked in front of the desk. The hum reached an unbearable pitch and I felt like I was simultaneously falling and rising at great speed. He looked at me. On his face was a mixed look of elation, triumph, wonder, fear and comprehension. He opened his mouth, as if to speak, but instead looked to the left. And then ... how does one explain the inexplicable? How does one describe the indescribable?

An incredible brightness illuminated him from the left. It was the starkest light I had ever seen but, strangely, it didn't hurt my eyes to look at it. From being a solid human body, Kanton suddenly, and at once, became a dimensionally flat object, like a cardboard popup in a book. But it was only for a moment. Then - and there is no other way to describe this - the book slammed shut. He folded in the middle, into himself, and disappeared. The humming stopped.

I screamed; I'm not ashamed to admit it. It was all so very unexpected and unreal. For a few moments, I was unable to comprehend what had just happened. Dr Reynolds had fallen to his knees, his face buried in his hands. I could not tell if he was praying or simply overcome. That was when I began shouting for the housekeeper and the police.

Emmanuel Kanton has not been seen since, nor any trace of him found. The police investigated but, given his previous mental history, they did not pursue it very far. I was required to give a statement, and here I must apologise.

It is not my custom to lie to the police; but, in view of what I had seen and heard and, in light of what Dr. Reynolds and I discovered after the fact, I felt it my Christian duty.

The police believe that, under mental strain, or a resurgence of schizophrenia, Emmanuel simply left the house and disappeared, like so many who disappear each year. They even suggested that, under this strain, he had drowned himself in the nearby river, or gone to the coast and thrown himself into the sea. They were fully expecting his body to turn up at any time. I did try at first in vain, to explain what had happened. I could have pointed out that pile of thin, bluish grey dust in front of the desk and demanded they analyse it. I was sure it would prove to be all that was left of the last mortal remains of Emmanuel Kanton. But, oddly enough, the cat pushed open the door to the garden just after he disappeared and the wind blowing in from the stormy day scattered and dispersed the dust in seconds, so that nothing remained. I've always wondered if that was purely coincidental.

When the police had left, Dr. Reynolds and I examined the contents of the study, leaving the desk for last. I pointed out to him the spot where the blue grey dust had, for a moment, rested. He looked at me gravely and then, kneeling, traced the sign of the cross over the spot and murmured a psalm.

We examined the desk. It was still covered in drawings, notes and equations that meant nothing to us. At the top of the desk, we found the little black, leatherbound book that Emanuel had cited as his inspiration. It was pinned open at a particular page and a red plastic pointer rested on one side, highlighting a particular verse.

On seeing it, Dr. Reynolds turned pale. He looked at me and his eyes rapidly flickered over the box, the notes, and the equations. Suddenly, I knew what the face of the Apostle Paul must have looked like, when he returned from his visions, having been called up to the Third Heaven, where he had heard all manner of spiritual things of which it was not lawful to speak.

'I must pray,' said Dr. Reynolds hoarsely, and stumbled out into the night. Although it was Summer, I lit a fire in the grate, against the protests of the housekeeper. I sent her away and then, methodically, burnt all the notes and drawings I could find, even burning some of the books. I then took a screwdriver and hammer and disassembled and destroyed every mechanical and electrical component I could find. I was determined that no one should ever duplicate Emmanuel's work or attempt to build on it.

Poor Dr Reynolds didn't last very long; he went from bad to worse and had to give up his duties at the university. One morning, he was found at the foot of the cliffs on the seashore with a striking expression on his face, as though he had escaped from some great trouble. He was buried quietly and that was that. No one linked his death with Kanton's disappearance.

I continued working at the university; I am not ambitious and it was pleasant enough. One day I got a call from my friend Adelia. She often organised sales of antiques and curios and knew of my interest in such things. She explained that her next sale would be of geological specimens and there would be a good range. I went to see her. Although my house was filled with many such objects, I could always find room for a particularly interesting example.

I wandered around the various stalls but found nothing that made me want to reach for my wallet, until I reached Adelia's stall. When I told her that I hadn't found anything, she smiled.

'I may have something,' she said teasingly. 'I know you don't often buy laboratory-created crystals, but this one's unusual enough that it may just pique your interest.'

She gestured to the back of the stall where an object was

covered with a red cloth.

'I've been keeping it for you,' she said happily. 'It's a quartz crystal, created using a new technique. It's beautifully clear but, in the centre there's that milkiness you get in quartz; in this instance it's formed a simulacrum, an image of something. It's not like those ones where you have to squint to see it; it's really quite clear.'

She pulled off the cloth with a flourish and my heart almost stopped. A roaring began in my ears and I was only dimly aware of Adelia asking if I felt ok. There, in the heart of the crystal, the milky cloud had formed an image; a very clear image, albeit a little distorted. I whispered to myself a paraphrase of the line we had read, in the little black book on Kanton's desk, that fateful morning. It was from Genesis, chapter four, verse nine: "And Emmanuel walked with God and he was NOT: for God took him."

I bought the crystal and kept it on the shelf above my desk.

Now, when I read a story about how scientists are about to push the boundaries of knowledge without knowing what the outcome will be, I look up at the crystal on the shelf. There, in the heart of the crystal matrix, is the face of Emmanuel Kanton, a little twisted, as though in constant agony; his eyes wild, mouth open.

It is as if he is trying to shout something.

HARIX

By Anthony Laken

He was squinting again; I guess it was because he spent all his day in front of the computer screen. It was ten thirty in the morning and I had just got up. A cup of coffee was steaming in my hand and I rested my arm across the top of his monitor. I yawned, not bothering to cover my mouth.

'Do you mind, Stenson?' he snapped, trying to shoo my hand away.

'No, I don't mind. How about you, Grass?'

Grass fixed me with the squint. I knew it meant piss off. I decided it was too early to get into one and shuffled away.

I meandered to my work desk and sat down, drawing my dressing gown around me tightly, crossed one leg over the other and leant back in my chair. The computer on my desk was covered in a thin layer of dust. I thought about wiping it down but decided against it. In the reflection of the screen I caught a glimpse of myself. My hair had grown long and a rather fine beard covered my face. I gave it a stroke and pretended I was a dashing cavalier; an effect slightly ruined by the curry stains on the front of my shirt.

Letting out a sigh I spun on my cheap office chair and faced the window. The snow was falling deep and hard on the moon of Harix, just like it had been for the past six months. It would continue to fall for two more yet, and that's when the heroes of the expedition would return.

Mapping the great unknown, plunging headfirst into danger. It was an attractive call to many people my age, sick of watching Earth die. Frankly I was only interested in the paycheque. Eight months of nothing to do but stare out the window and count the snowflakes. It was my idea of heaven.

For guys like Grass however, it was a snub from the bosses. He thought he should be the one standing on the front of the snow plough, rappelling down the mountains and extracting the precious Gordium from the cliffs. Instead, his test had conclusively consigned him to babysitting databanks and monitors.

I thought of the first day we'd met at the handover. Grass had stood to attention like he had a rod up his arse while the departing heroes laughed at him. For a few minutes I felt sorry for the guy and made a stab at civil conversation. Grass had looked me up and down and condemned our future relationship by declaring my tie to be against regulations. It was at that point I had decided to make his life as uncomfortable as possible.

To be fair though, I didn't have to try very hard. The very fact I existed drove Grass into states of nervous exhaustion. The way I ate, the way I shaved, how I folded my clothes; all of these things had become a battlefield of triviality as the landscape outside our window disappeared in a blanket of white.

'Why do you do this to yourself, Grass?' I said before taking a satisfying swig of my coffee which I'd made Irish, despite the early hour.

'Do what?' came the little man's response.

'Keep looking every day? You know there ain't nothing gonna turn up,'

'That's where you're wrong, Stenson. I'm going to be the first person to locate that tunnel and ride the rocket of praise outta here,'

'How the hell are you gonna find anything out there? I can tell you right now what the cameras on the drones are picking up: white, white and a smidge more white. Am I wrong?'

'Shut up, Stenson! I'm trying to concentrate.'

The video feed from the drones was reflected in his glasses. Guess what - it was white.

I rummaged on my desk for a half-eaten pack of biscuits and unearthed a photo of my ex. She had taken the bold move of breaking up with me via a time-delayed text. In the photo, everything was still going good. It was from the lovely period before I'd started to grate on her nerves. We had both thought the job on Harix would be good for our relationship. I realised now it was a good opportunity for her to move in with that snake in the grass, Philbert.

I pushed the photo back under the mountain of rubbish on my desk and decided my coffee could handle being a touch more Irish. As my slippers slapped out a mournful tune on the wooden floor, Grass gave an excited squeak.

'Ha ha! Take that, Schofield-Phillips aptitude test! Who's an ideal office maintainer now?

'Don't tell me you found it? All the scouts, the high tech gear and a satellite sweep couldn't find that stupid tunnel!' I said scurrying over.

'Well they're clearly no match for Colin Grass,' he replied with a triumphant raising of his specs.

I stared past his shoulder at the screen. My mouth hung open in disbelief. There it was, right where the last transmission from Colonel Ferric had come from.

Why now? I asked myself. Why hadn't anyone found it in three months of searching in perfect conditions?

'We need to call this in Grass, right now,' I said reaching over to the communication console. Grass pushed my hand aside.

'How about we go and have a little look for ourselves?' Grass said, eyes glinting.

Now, as you may have gathered, honour, glory and all that crap doesn't really motivate me. But finding that photo had got my blood running hot and in the opposite direction from my brain. What a way to show Melinda and Philbert, I thought. Man, was that a mistake.

Thirty minutes later, amidst the debris of two men scrambling in snow for the first time, I stood face to face with Grass. Over his pale white face was a helmet, tucked beyond which was his muffler. He nodded at me with greedy eyes. I opened the garage shutter and prayed to all the gods we'd be fine.

I'd checked the weather satellite before we left. It had seemed good, well as good as it got on Harix, which meant the snowfall would be merely hard instead of a blizzard. Good god, it was cold though. In the whole eight months at the research station, neither of us had set foot outside once. Despite layers of the best protective gear money could buy, I was still shivering. It was with trembling hands I fired up the snowmobile; I tried to convince myself it was all down to the chill.

Grass hopped on the back of his vehicle and took the lead. There was no real reason as we both had satnavs between the handlebars, but I thought I'd throw the guy a bone, let him feel like he was in charge. Also, if anything popped out and decided to eat us, I thought I'd get a few seconds warning.

The sky was a dirty grey colour, an old t-shirt in need of a wash, as we set off into the valley. Along the way, my mind ran back to the story of the tunnel. It wasn't one that filled me with confidence, especially now that the rush of blood had passed. I wondered what the hell I was doing.

The incident had occurred three months prior to our arrival on Harix. Colonel Ferric had set off on one of his famous jaunts into the mountains. He was ludicrously posh and had spent a lifetime adventuring while the rest of us had to get real jobs. This, of course, meant he wasn't a conventional colonel but had been assigned the rank by Quark Industries - they thought it best if the scouts they sent had some basic military training and ranks to maintain discipline. In essence, it meant that a lot of people with more money than sense could buy their positions on these planetary pioneer missions.

I digress. So anyway, off he had gone. He had been out for five hours when base had received a garbled message concerning a tunnel. I'd heard the recording and, the best you could say about it was that Ferric was excited, though hysterical would be closer to the mark. Something about markings and possible Aurumvanti remains. Any hint of that race of ancient beings is enough to send the world into a spin. Obviously, Quark were more than a little interested.

Unfortunately for them that was when all contact with the Colonel had been lost. All that was left was the message and a set of coordinates. And no one was able to find even a hint of Ferric or the tunnel. Which was why now, in the cold slap of Harix, I began to have my doubts. I pushed it to the back of my mind and tried to focus - I saw Melinda crying into a handkerchief as I was handed a medal; it was petty but it kept me going.

Through the wall of snow that was now falling, I saw Grass hold up his hand for us to stop. It was actually a good thing 'cause I had been so out of it even the satnav's incessant whine had escaped me. Hopping down from my snowmobile I walked around like John Wayne, until my thighs felt normal again. Grass meanwhile was all business.

He held his satnav in his hand and was searching for the tunnel opening we had both seen on the monitor back at base. Even from a distance I could tell he was upset. I wandered over and saw what was troubling him: the tunnel wasn't there.

'What the hell is this, Grass?' I asked through our comlinks.

'I don't know. We should be right on top of it!'

I sighed and looked around. Huge mountains rose on both sides of us, making me feel like an amoeba gazing up at a more complex life form. Somehow Harix seemed alive, something ancient and knowing.

I sat down on the snowmobile and left Grass to his fevered search. Suddenly the ground began to shake and a grinding noise like a ship running aground filled the air. It was a sound I'd heard before but couldn't quite place. A wall of snow rushed towards me. My body froze. There was nothing I could do.

Out of nowhere, a spike of rock shot out from the ground in front of me. The avalanche exploded against it, causing snow to cascade around its sides in a white waterfall. At some point I'd fallen to my knees. I struggled back to my feet, and felt a horrible warmth trickle down my leg. Thankfully Grass was in a pretty similar position. He was crouched down, beside where the rock had burst out of the ground - a few inches to the left and he would have been a human shish kebab.

'How in the world?' I said, walking towards the rock that had saved our lives. I couldn't be sure but it seemed as if the landscape was different; like it had all shifted ever so slightly to the left.

'Never mind that, look!' Grass exclaimed.

I followed his shaking finger with my eyes: the tunnel had appeared again. Grass hurried towards it, unconcerned with the sheer scale of weirdness that was befalling us.

'Grass, hold up! That's enough, man. We found the tunnel so let's just get outta here and call this in!'

He wasn't listening. He quickly paused before the gaping mouth of the tunnel, then ran inside. In my mind I was battling with curiosity and fear. Something wasn't right. I could feel it. Fear won out and I positioned my numb arse back on the snowmobile. Now you can think what you want about me leaving Grass; my survival instinct had kicked in and I had no love for the guy.

I fired up my vehicle and set off, but didn't get far. In front of me another finger of rock shot into the sky. Frantically I swerved out of its way. More and more appeared, fencing me in and forcing me back towards the tunnel entrance. I sat before the opening, my heart trying its best to smash through my ribcage. The stones looked down at me and, in that strange atmosphere, I thought I sensed pity in them. I was completely surrounded. The only open path left was the one leading into the tunnel.

The opening gaped before me, a whale ready to swallow its Jonah. I felt a pull in my mind to go inside. It was intoxicating; like the pull of drunken feet to the dance floor. Where the snow had fallen away around the tunnel, the rock of Harix was now fully exposed. It was the colour of a new purple-blue bruise and had the appearance of a punched eye.

I peered into the darkness and swallowed hard. It was pitch black so I flipped on my helmet's lamp. One hundred watts of light ballooned out and created a clutch of menacing shadows. I stood on the threshold and tried to get hold of Grass on my comlink. All I got in return was static. I'm no tech whizz but I knew the comlinks were supposed to be nigh on infallible, so I took the electronic hiss as a very bad sign.

On reluctant feet, I stepped inside. The rocks around me glistened with the veins of Gordium and made the stones seem like boils. Despite the cold outside, I found myself sweating in the mouth of the tunnel and took my face-guard off. I took a sniff of the air and wished I hadn't bothered. A fetid stench threatened to infest my nostrils and stop me smelling anything decent ever again. I retched and said a small prayer of thanks that I hadn't got round to my usual breakfast of the previous night's reheated curry.

I stumbled on into the tunnel and found it growing wider. Blue lights flickered into existence at regular intervals along the walls. Scattered across their surface, illuminated in pale blue, was a historian's lifetime work in Aurumvanti wall art. It stretched on and on with every step I took, completely eclipsing anything ever found before. I mean, I'd seen the photos and diagrams in textbooks back on Earth but nothing like this. It was breathtaking and terrifying all at once.

All that was known about the Aurumvanti was that they had got there first. For every human accomplishment we could list, they had beaten us to it. Then, bam, nothing. They had disappeared into the mists of time. There had been vague references to a race of creature called the Silvolgus but nothing to pin your hat on. What I learned from the wall carvings was probably more than a thousand eggheads had worked out in a hundred years. The Aurumvanti language was pictorial and these images, strung out in regulated squares like an alien comic strip, gave me a glimpse at their fate.

Of course, a fair bit of what I saw was highly symbolic and I didn't have the skills to decipher it. But then you don't really need to a have a degree in weird shit to understand the meaning of insect-like creatures devouring a planet of screaming Aurumvanti. In the few glimpses of the Silvolgus in other Aurumvanti art the creatures had been small, about waist high on the humanoid Aurums. But here they had taken on a monumental scale. The last frieze depicted a ship of Aurumvanti departing into space. After that there was nothing. So they floated off to escape the giant cockroaches, I thought; what then?

My musing didn't last long as I heard a shriek from further ahead. It was a type of cry I'd heard countless times before, usually when I'd committed some grievous sin like mixing colours in the washing machine. It was Grass and he was clearly distraught.

I hurried forward and found my fellow caretaker backed into a corner by what I could only describe as a moving pile of rock. It stood about four feet tall and was connected by a glowing orange core. The colour spread out from its stomach and along it limbs. Grass was huddled in a ball shivering but my gut told me the walking pile of rubble meant no harm. In fact I think it was trying to take his coat. By now I'd completely removed my helmet, and I saw Grass had done the same.

'Get this thing away from me, Stenson!' Grass cried. The rock man turned to look at me.

'Calm down, Grass! For goodness sake, if it wanted to hurt you I'm sure it would've by now.'

The creature approached me and plucked my discarded clothes and gear from my hand. It performed a little bow then scuttled off.

'See, it was trying to be helpful,' I said.

'Yeah just like I'm sure they "helped" Colonel Ferric,' Grass replied.

'Oh but they did help me!' A voice reverberated around the tunnel.

'Who the hell's there?' Grass called out. Obviously he hadn't paid enough attention to the Colonel's last transmission, otherwise he would have placed it straight away, like I had.

'Follow the lights and all will be revealed,' Ferric intoned.

At that point all I wanted to do was go back to base and drown myself in a sea of beer, vindaloo and porn, but I knew the sentient rocks had other ideas.

'C'mon Grass,' I said, pulling him to his feet.

'You can't be serious, Stenson?! We need to get back to base!'

'Trust me, there's no way back to base. Let's go and get to the bottom of this. Hey, you never know, we might even live long enough to regret it.' I left Grass to his whispered curses. The glistening lights increased suddenly in their intensity along the tunnel, leaving an afterburn on my retinas. It looked like it would be a long walk.

I was wrong on that count, and I was grateful for that. About fifteen minutes later, Grass and I were standing in a cavernous space. The path we followed had mushroomed and the room we found ourselves in now was more like a citadel. The rock on either side of us plunged down in a vertigo-inducing swirl. It was like looking at one of those pictures where you have to go cross-eyed to see the rabbit hidden in the pattern. Several struts and gangways arched out to a central platform, a gargantuan piece of chiselled Gordium.

Around us the rock men scuttled, carrying loads of harvested Gordium. They seemed happy enough and were careful to veer out of our way. One found us staring dumbfounded at the space and waited. With dazzled eyes I turned my head towards it. All this shit was hidden beneath the ground of Harix? Why in the name of all that was good had no one discovered it before? I mean, the ground was impossibly hard to dig into, but surely there should have been something?

The little guy let out a series of beeps and zoomed ahead, then paused and turned back towards us.

'I think it wants us to follow,' Grass said.

'No shit,' I replied.

We followed it out over a balcony of rock that would have given a health and safety inspector a fit. It was about three feet wide and plunged down into that friendly abyss I mentioned before. We were led to the Gordium platform and up its narrow steps. At the top we found ourselves face to face with Colonel Ferric.

His pale blonde hair hung limply in front of his eyes and a beard that would have impressed a hermit covered his jaw. He lifted his head solemnly and regarded us like a king.

'So you have been chosen to share the secrets of the Aurumvanti?' he said.

'Well if your definition of chosen is to be herded by moving stones then, yeah I s'pose we have,' I replied.

'You are glib, the Masters will not like that!' Ferric said.

'Forgive him, oh mighty lord, he knows nothing of what he does,' Grass added.

'Yes, you are more suitable,' Ferric said looking down his nose at Grass, 'I'm sure the Masters will have a fitting job for you. We have many things that need looking after,'

Grass's face fell at this and I suppressed a laugh. It didn't last long though. Ferric began to pace up and down his little platform, scratching his face and pulling on his beard, muttering all the while.

'Why? Why them, oh glorious ones? They are weak and foolish,' he moaned into the air like a hammy actor. He cocked his head to one side and appeared to be listening. Every now and then he nodded and licked his lips. Finally a look of the greatest epiphany passed across his face. 'I see! Yes of course. How could I ever have doubted you?' Ferric called into the ether. 'You two, follow me.' He crooked his finger at us and then set off.

A rubble dude met us at the start of another walkway and led us along. At this point, some part of me was finding this all a little amusing. What Ferric said next changed that.

'We are to be the sacrifices that awaken the Masters from their slumber. In half an hour, we shall die and they will live again!' as the Colonel spoke, spittle flew from his mouth and flecked his chin. His eyes bulged and his body shook. Great, I thought, he's fucking nuts. I looked at Grass and for the first time we understood each other.

'Oh this is an honour unfit for ones as lowly as us,' Grass said.

'Yeah we really should be heading back to base, Colonel. Why don't you come with us?' I said.

'Leave?' the Colonel spat, rounding on me. 'Leave? Why in the name of the great sky gods would I leave? They have shown me things. Wonders that we could only dream of. To the Masters we are but dust in the wind. They must rise again and defeat the Devourers!'

'That would be the Silvolgus, wouldn't it?' I said, 'But they're gone, just like the Aurumvanti are,'

'That's where you're wrong, where we were all wrong. They are merely waiting, hiding in the gaps between realities to strike, just like they did before. They will come and bring their hunger. Then a silence will descend upon us, and our colonies will be lost as they feast,'

By this point my mind was reeling. The colonel had lost his senses, that much was sure, but then I didn't know really what level of sanity a man who had spent five months underground, with only rock guys for company, should possess. How the hell was I supposed to get out of this? For the moment I decided to play along and hope that at some point we'd get the chance to make a break for it.

On and on, along tunnels lined with Gordium we traipsed. Even though Ferric looked like he had been living on a steady diet of moss, he moved at a ferocious pace. Soon we arrived in another vast chamber. It was circular and, at its centre sat a control panel with lots of levers that looked like it should have a big 'Do not touch' sign over it. Much to my dismay, Ferric strolled over to it and began to fiddle with it. Around the walls of the chamber, what looked like monitors made of pure light popped up. I wandered over to one and examined the image it was displaying. There in front of me was our base. In the corner of my eye I saw Grass come up beside me.

'What the hell do we do, Stenson?' he hissed.

'How the hell should I know? We should be sitting in our rooms, snug and warm with a beer in one hand and our dicks in the other,' I said jabbing at the screen. 'But you had to come out here and have a look, didn't you? Rocket of praise, my arse! You bought us front row seats to a mental breakdown.'

Grass squinted at me. He was thinking, probably mentally skimming the Quark Industry handbook to see if there was a section on what to do if you're about to be killed by a deranged co-worker. Obviously there was nothing, as he let out a sigh.

'Goddammit - there has to be something we can do!' he said.

'For now, let's go along with it.'

'Typical Stenson. I should've known your solution would be to do nothing,'

'Screw you man! If we'd carried on doing nothing like we're paid to, we wouldn't be here!' I replied, jabbing him in the chest.

Grass shoved me away and I pushed him back. We began to flap our arms at each other like a couple of teenage girls fighting over lip-gloss. It wasn't my finest hour.

'Silence!' Ferric boomed from the centre of the room. 'The Master wishes to speak with you.'

We both turned and saw a giant holographic head floating above the consoles. Its face was smooth and white and looked like an ancient Greek statue come to life. It gazed down at us with disdain and I suddenly felt incredibly small.

I was beginning to wonder how it would speak when two orbs of light floated out from the head and wove their way to us. One of the spheres paused before my eyes then shot toward my face. My brain exploded with light, and a blur of images flashed through my mind at a rate of knots. Alien planets, great towering cities, people enjoying a land of plenty. Then the Silvolgus appeared. The wall art I had seen earlier did not do them justice. They had first gone unnoticed, little more than big locusts with fangs. But they had grown. Whole harvests were devoured; cities fell crumbling as the Silvolgus ate the very stone they were made from.

The Aurumvanti had tried to flee but the Silvolgus had a nasty trick up their sleeves. An image that I knew would stay with me to my dying day filled my mind. I saw a small child by his mother's side. He collapsed to the ground as his skin rippled and bulged. What happened next is hard to describe, but imagine a straw being plunged into a person and them being sucked dry. The withered husk of the child fell apart like confetti and, from this shell, a Silvolgus emerged.

I thought I was going to be sick; at that point I wasn't sure I hadn't. The tiny part of my brain not being bombarded prayed for it to end. Instead I was shown Harix. The Aurumvanti had built it. They had built the moon we stood on. A lab appeared and I was shown Aurum scientists experimenting on a captured Silvolgus. After this, I saw it eat one of its own. They had genetically engineered a cannibal. My mind was filled with an image of row upon row of this new breed of Silvolgus incubating in the heart of Harix. The Aurums who had conducted these experiments fed themselves into a machine that reduced them to mush. This was pumped via tubes as sustenance for the Silvolgus.

As suddenly as the worst slide show ever had started in my head, it finished. I collapsed to the floor, retching and struggling for air. With my face pressed against the floor, eyelids flickering, I vaguely noticed Grass lying prostate beside me.

'Now do you see? The time has come for the children born of this fake moon to fly and save us all!' Ferric boomed. My head throbbed and I wondered why posh people always seemed to have such loud voices.

'But the Silvolgus have gone, Ferric, and so have the Aurumvanti! Whatever they were trying to do here, they failed,' I shouted, forcing myself upright.

Ferric seemed perturbed by this and, for a second, a look of indecision flickered across his face. Then, to my horror, his skin began to bubble and writhe. The head behind him smiled. The eyes on its face had turned black. Something was very wrong.

Then it struck me: the Silvolgus were controlling the Aurumvanti as well as eating them from the inside.

'Oh god no!' Grass exclaimed, pointing a trembling finger at Ferric. 'They're gonna burst outta him like that kid!'

'Fuck this. Grass we've gotta move, as in five minutes ago!'

I grabbed Grass by the arm and ran. Behind us, the giant head let out a strange whinnying sound - it was laughing. We hurried along the tunnels, not looking back. We had just found our way back to the entrance when the rock guys' big brother showed up. It stood about six feet high, glistening with Gordium crystals. It made a dash for us and I pushed Grass to the left. A giant fist slammed into the floor and a crack splintered around it like a snowflake. It rounded on me and I backed up until I hit the wall. My body refused to do react and I stood there like an idiot waiting for the end.

Just as it reached me, the crystal monster jerked unexpectedly backwards; Grass was hanging from its back, his pickaxe lodged in its skull. The thing flailed around, trying to grab hold of him.

'Go!' he screamed at me.

'Grass, I can't just...'

'Do it! Get back to base and initiate Protocol Fifteen,'

With that, the monster fell on its back and rolled down the tunnel. There was a sickening sound, like the one my dog used to make when it cracked open a bone to get at the marrow, and I knew Grass had been smashed to pieces.

Finally my brain and body reached an agreement and my legs moved faster than I ever thought they could. I crashed out into the snowy waste of Harix and felt the cold slap my face. Cursing, I remembered that one of the small rock guys had taken my helmet and face-mask.

The rocks that had previously shot out of the ground were

still there, but I now noticed a gap between them I thought I could squeeze through on the snowmobile. I jumped into the seat and fired her up. With a twist of my wrist the machine roared to life and barrelled towards the opening. The gap was just wide enough but I could see the stone fingers on either side of me trying to squeeze together. I managed to burst through but the snowmobile took a knock.

The engine coughed and spluttered its way back to base. How, I do not know. I once had a car back on Earth that was an unmitigated pile of crap. But I swear that thing had a mind of its own and it made journeys you never would have thought possible. I had loved that car and in that moment I loved that snowmobile.

I drove straight into the garage, closed the shutters and sprinted for the control room. I booted up my computer and frantically sought out the post-it I'd written my log-in details on: "MeLinDa&StEve4Life". I chuckled at that, in spite of myself. The screen popped open - I had three thousand unread emails. Those penis-enlarging pills would have to wait, I told myself, and began searching for Quark Industry's Protocol book. It didn't take me long to locate Protocol Fifteen. I wished I hadn't.

It was a planet-wide scorched earth policy in case of contamination of an unknown kind. According to the manual, I could instigate it from my PC; it was a drastic measure but, from what I'd seen in the caverns beneath Harix, I knew it was necessary. A few clicks later and it was done. I turned away from the computer and started to prep the emergency shuttle. It wouldn't get me back home but it should've been sufficient for getting me away from Harix with a distress signal blaring. Unfortunately that never happened.

My PC beeped and the screen flashed red. I ran back over to see what the problem was. There had been a malfunction in the Masood Engine and I needed to replace the Frink piston. At that point, I'm not ashamed to say, I wept. Where the hell could I find one of those? Then the answer arrived: I could take the one from the engine of the escape shuttle.

I'm not a hero. All I had ever wanted was a simple life doing nothing. A decision like this was for the Ferrics of the world to make. There was no telling if the Silvolgus would actually make it off Harix, I told myself when I was halfway to the shuttle doors. But then I remembered the Aurumvanti worlds falling, and the child being eaten from the inside. At that point I didn't think of my family or my country or even Melinda; I thought of Broadstairs beach. I've lost count of the amount of summers my family spent there on the sands, laughing and swimming, ice creams melting beneath the one day of sunshine in England that year. Then I saw the Silvolgus swarming across it, devouring everything in their path and I knew what I had to do.

So here I sit in the basement of the control room, watching the timer count down. I've broadcast this on all available frequencies and I hope to god someone hears it. Not for my sake but for Colin Grass, the bravest guy I ever met.

Ha. I just got a text from Melinda. She wants to try again.

WITH MY EVERY BREATH

By K.J. Lymer

Despite it being 4 o' clock in the afternoon, it is already dusk and the municipal gas lamps are flickering into flame along the street, accentuating the row of fashionable hats on display in the shop window. But this is no ordinary salon – it is the exclusive outlet for the designs of the celebrated chapelier Louis LeBlanc, which is situated in the Arcadian quarter of Torontopolis. Chiefs, queens, politicians and the upper classes of Neo-Canadian society have all sought his high couture hats, while I have waited all day with nervousness to visit this famous millinery.

My father, Professor Euan Warnock, takes my arm in his with a solid grip. Even though his white frilled shirt and outer black jacket cover his right arm, I can still feel its cold metal surface.

'Alice, come my dear, it is time,' he says, and yanks me in his impatience. I stumble as I try to keep up with his brisk pace.

We enter the shop and a small bell rings above the door. My eyes adjust to the dim light of the gaslight chandelier. Hats of different sizes, shapes and colours overflow the room. In one corner there are beaver-fur D'Orsays, which are similar to the top hat my father wears, along with high-crown bowlers that are the latest fashion to come from Europe. The men's section, however, is nothing in comparison with the marvellous selection of hats for women – so many that I can't even begin to describe them. I stare in awe at the multitude of colours, shapes and styles.

'You, miss, I seek a hat for my daughter,' demands my

father, his Scottish inflection unmistakable.

A middle-aged clerk in a grey, pinstriped dress approaches us. She wears a leather patch over her left eye from which a monocular eyepiece is attached. 'What is Mademoiselle looking for?' Her French accent is conspicuous, but not strong. Her dress is one that I had not seen before and I can't identify what part of French Neo-Canada she comes from.

She scrutinises me with a cold stare while her eyepiece extends forward with a whirl and a click. She probably does not like my appearance – a pallid sixteen-year-old girl with mismatched eyes of hazel and blue – but I am quite used to people being disturbed by my cadaverous appearance. Sometimes, I just want to scream, 'Yes, I am the walking dead, damn it!' But then, it is best they don't know my dark secret, and not to mention the fact that father would punish me for such an indiscretion.

On second thought, perhaps she doesn't like the plain grey cloak covering my simple black dress. I am not clothed in the height of fashion, as it is difficult to buy new clothes against father's penny-pinching disapprovals.

Father nudges me forward. I stare straight into the clerk's disconcerting mechanical eye and see the reflection of my face and my braided Venetian blond hair in its dark lens. I beam my warmest smile. 'Something with feathers, if you please, miss.'

She turns away to find a hat. Father points with a sharp gesture towards the direction of the lever lock keys on a ring, similar to the ones that hang from her waist, dangling by the cash register.

'Perhaps this one,' she suggests, and grabs a small black hat with a long grouse tail feather.

'N-no,' I stammer. 'I am looking for something more exotic – I do love rare birds deriving from dark and distant countries.'

I watch Father move to a dark corner. He rolls up his

right sleeve and switches on the Cryptobiotic Aura Spectral Scanner (CASS) set within his brass forearm. The dials light up and he dons special glasses that sync with the CASS to identify cryptoid signatures.

My father is the proud inventor of the CASS, which identifies the unique auras of cryptoids, as he calls those strange beasts. I have heard him boast to his scientific colleagues on many occasions that these are extraordinary creatures possessing a portmanteau of different body parts, like the fur-bearing trouts of Sault Ste. Marie or the fabulous creatures of mythology, such as gryphons and unicorns. It has become his great obsession to hunt down cryptoids, as he gave up his medical studies in faraway Scotland to become a professor of cryptozoology at an institute in Torontopolis.

Father struts around the showroom and then comes to an abrupt stop. I know the CASS has found nothing by the way he addresses the clerk with an air of haughty annoyance. 'Miss, let's be blunt – we're looking for gryphon feathers.'

She replies in a tone that doesn't disguise the contempt she holds for my father. 'Gryphons? I am sorry monsieur, we do not stock creatures from *contes de fées*, fairy-tales. Perhaps, I may suggest visiting the toy emporium down the street?'

'I demand to speak with your proprietor!' Father enjoys being belligerent to people who are beneath his esteem – there is a mischievous glint in his eyes as he removes his glasses. I edge towards the cash register.

The clerk glares at my father with a stare bitterer than a buffuloberry. 'Monsieur LeBlanc is not here. Now leave or I shall have to call the constabulary.'

'Then, good day to you, madam,' retorts father. He beckons me with a gesture from his shiny brass hand and I scurry to his side before facing his displeasure. We leave the premise without father making any more theatrics.

As we march away from the shop, father enquires in a

gruff whisper, "Did you obtain them?'

I pull from my hidden pocket the key ring, which I had only snatched a few minutes ago. I jingle the lever locks and secrete them back undercover again.

At Father's insistence, I had been trained in the art of stealth and pick pocketing by master thieves only a few months after my resurrection – I had just turned fifteen when I died in a tragic accident. One year on, my home schooling included mathematics, chemistry and history, while father was adamant that I learned the Japanese shinobi skills of espionage and sabotage, which are conducted by my governess Yoshiko. Therefore, our visit to the millinery was not to purchase a fashionable hat for me – though I wished we did – but in pursuit of a tantalising clue about gryphon feathers …

Last evening, Father had attended a high society event at the Royal Victoria Hotel in the city centre. Around midnight he returned and burst into the parlour downstairs. I came out of my bedroom and looked down to the ground floor below. I had not seen him so excited in such a long time.

'I have had a productive evening, despite it being full of dullards and cretins from the political classes and aristocracy,' he proclaimed, while removing his cloak and top hat. He was addressing Yoshiko, who was conducting her Zen meditations in the parlour. He smiled when I entered into the room to join them.

'The reception was a cumbersome affair and the amateur chamber quartet was full of tone-deaf minstrels, but it was saved by my accidental encounter with the Ketwatian First Princess. Her father, the Supreme First Chief, was there shaking hands and trying to grab more land for the Autonomous Ketwatin Province, no doubt.'

I watched my father pour himself a glass of expensive imported Scottish whisky.

'I presented my scholarly credentials to her and engaged her with erudite conversation full of fanciful scientific proposals, such as the possibility of capturing thunderbirds for her to tame as pets.' He paused and lit a cigar. 'It is always good to cultivate potential patrons for the institute.' He smirked and gave me a wink.

He continued, 'She was dressed in the height of fashion. A shawl of bird feathers draped over her shoulders, which almost looked like wings. But the most extraordinary thing was her feathered headdress – the design was a mix between traditional Athabascan costume and Parisian couture.

'My CASS quietly buzzed on my arm and I scrutinised the headdress. The princess caught my gaze and proceeded to tell me that it was designed by the noted Arcadian hatter, Louis LeBlanc, who had managed to obtain the finest golden eagle feathers; believed to hold the power of spirits among the pagan beliefs of her people.

'I was more than pleased to point out that two of her crown feathers were not eagle. The princess smiled and gently stroked them. "Oh, yes, I think Monsieur LeBlanc called them 'griff-on' – a rare Asiatic bird of great wisdom", she confided with me. I asked the princess if I could take a polychrome of her headdress with my Maddox microplate camera and then bade her farewell.'

Father paused. He sipped his glass and turned to stare at me. 'Tomorrow we must find out where the Arcadian hatter obtained these feathers. The implications are stupendous, especially if I can discover a new source of gryphons for my English benefactor. Moreover, this evidence may lead to another portal into a fantastic realm, so much like that one discovered by a young lass in England a few years ago.'

After the brief outing to the millinery in the afternoon, I spend the evening making preparations with Yoshiko for an undercover mission. She is a small, unassuming woman with deep hazel eyes, who fights with feline ferocity. She does not talk much, but speaks perfect English in a soft voice. I, however, cannot consider her as a friend or confidant. Yoshiko is a taskmaster and sergeant-at-arms – always issuing orders and pointing out my faults. But for someone so skilled as a tactician and warrior, I can't understand how she came under Father's employ; though once I overheard a conversation that revealed she carries out her governess duties to pay off a mysterious debt.

Just before midnight we set out to the Arcadian quarter in an old steam cart driven by her. Not to attract any unwanted attention, we dress as coal merchants wearing plain woollen jackets and dark trousers. I tuck my single plait under a warm beaver-cap, while Yoshiko covers her head with a dark, shapeless hat.

As we pass through the narrow streets, I watch her manoeuvre this rackety vehicle. Shadows emphasise her gaunt facial lines and torn left ear. I am in no doubt that these features chronicle the battles which she has fought over the years.

We hit a pothole and I am thrown off my seat. Yoshiko slows down.

'Are you all right, Alice?'

I slip back onto the rock hard seat. 'Y-yes, I'm fine.'

As she returns to a higher gear, I notice the thin leather band around Yoshiko's neck from which hangs a bronze coin. A few months ago I had stumbled upon her trying to pull it off in the bathroom. She called it an accursed amulet and made me swear not to speak about it to anyone. As I reflect upon this incident, it proves she does trust me in keeping secrets to some degree.

The constant throbbing of the steam engine gives me a headache, while the coal cart's passenger seat hurts my back. A mood of unease sweeps through me and I feel a great compulsion to talk to Yoshiko, despite the fact there is still quite a chasm between us. I have no friends of my own age to converse with as father keeps me in the house with home schooling. I need someone to talk to. Anyone.

'Yoshiko? I can't bear my awful nightmare any longer – it came to me again last night.'

She doesn't respond and keeps her focus on navigating the steam cart through the labyrinth of dark avenues.

'The sleeping draught doesn't work any longer. But I can't tell Father for he just gets angry and dismisses me like some dim-witted child.'

Yoshiko turns her head away from the steering wheel to look at me. I take this as silent approval to carry on.

'I have had it for over a year now. Most of the time the dream follows the same scenario – I'm crying in bed and hugging my favourite stuffed toy. Someone, or something, enters my room and stabs me in the chest. Sometimes I am lying on a hospital bed, a creaky old mattress, or even in a mouldy coffin! The type of weapon is always unidentifiable – but it possesses an unusual shape as if it was a scythe, and shines like alabaster while it is being plunged into my heart. I am then swept away with such indescribable sensations of pain that it makes me wake up screaming.'

I lay my hand my chest close to my heart and feel the ridges of a large scar, even through the multiple layers of my clothes.

We turn a sharp corner, but this time I am prepared and steady myself.

'But why do I dream? I thought sleeping and having dreams is what separates the living from the undead? Well, at least that's what I think the natural order of things should be.'

Yoshiko doesn't reply. I now feel more cold and alone than the pale moon smothered in the dark velvet curtain of clouds that drift across the night sky.

The vehicle stops with a lurch and a rattle of rusting

gears. We kit up and march through several dark alleys to our destination.

Upon reaching the millinery, we scout around the vicinity. The lights are out in the building and the ground floor windows are locked and shuttered. Without a word Yoshiko gives the signal to begin our operation.

In the shadows I take my hat off to loosen my plait. The removal of my jacket reveals a dark corset with minute cogs and wheels. I release the locking mechanism on my right side and gossamer wings unfold from my back. Delicate gears whirl as the elaborate frame composed of carbon tempered bones locks into flight-position.

I take hold of the handles attached to the apex of the wing and start to run, then flap my arms vigorously and lift myself off the ground. It is an exhilarating feeling to fly. I marvel at my father's engineering skills for he refashioned these lightweight wing bones from an infantile jabberwocky into an aerodynamic glider.

I see from my lofty view Yoshiko entering the shop with the keys that I acquired several hours ago.

I glide like a sparrow, taking advantage of a gust of wind to land with precision on a third-floor windowsill. The frame slides open with ease and I enter a gloomy room. There is a sour odour in the air that reminds me of a tavern. I pull a lever to retract my wings and adjust my eyes to the darkness. It is a relief to enter into a hallway with dim-lit lamps that reveal the glint of liquor bottles littering the floor.

The soft glow of flames emanate from the entrance of the back room and the pungent aroma of burning cedar. I peer in and see the silhouette of a male figure standing in front of a marble fireplace. He empties a large teacup with a great slurp and fills it again with the remaining contents of a bottle. When he casts it aside, I see the label – Absinthe.

On the mantel of the fireplace there is glass box housing a large stuffed rattlesnake articulated in a striking pose by a taxidermist. The huge gaping mouth unsheathes two lethal white fangs – the very sight of them fills me with overwhelming fear. They have an uncanny resemblance to the alabaster scythe in my dream. A chill falls over me and I grasp my chest. The ridges of the scar near my heart feel like mountain peaks. I stagger and stumble over an empty bottle that rattles across the wooden floor. It knocks over a pile of bottles with a loud clatter.

'How did you get in here?' Like a serpent whose rocky den has just been overturned, the man seizes a neo-Webley Irish revolver off the table in a flutter of dislodged papers. 'Come in, so I can see you or I will shoot you dead!'

I recognise the seriousness of the situation, but at the same time I am also quite aware of my personal circumstances – I've already departed this mortal coil. I laugh nervously to myself.

I enter into the room with cautious steps. He closes the door and switches a table lamp to full brightness. I find myself staring at a small man with dishevelled brown hair wearing a white nightshirt that drapes over auburn trousers. His feet are bare and dirty as if he had walked over a pile of coals.

Behind him is a drafting board full of sketches exploring different hat designs. Large, dark oil paintings of natural landscapes hang from the walls. Sheets of paper are piled everywhere. I can also see his micro-Babbage engine drowned in a sea of documents on a solid oak table.

'Who are you?' His eyes move up and down me, while a wicked smile cracks across his face like ice breaking the surface of a muddy pond. 'Have you been sent by a jealous competitor to spy on Louis LeBlanc, my fillette? You are a strange looking girl, but very pretty. And what is that on your back? Such fine, delicate mechanical wings I see.'

I find his intense scrutiny unnerving.

'Who are you, my little chickadee?' LeBlanc pauses, then

without warning shouts, 'SPEAK!' – the savage ferocity of his voice makes me jump.

'I have come to find out where you acquired the gryphon feathers,' I splutter.

'Well, I'm not going to tell you, you silly little bird.'

He circles me, holding the revolver to my head. LeBlanc's blue eyes are wide as saucers and bloodshot, while his pupils are tiny dots. His breath stinks from the sour smell of fermented beverages.

He then screams, 'Gryphon feathers, chickadee feathers, winged girls without feathers – feathers, feathers, FEATHERS!'

This hatter is, in no doubt, quite mad – or at the very least already dancing at the edge of sanity. It is clear he will kill me at the slightest provocation. I need to draw my hand knife from its sheath tied to my right thigh.

I hear a loud click and the door bursts open. There is a blur as Yoshiko's tiger pounce knocks over LeBlanc and pins him to the floor. He wriggles and writhes for several minutes but she secures him in a tight hold.

I kneel down beside him on the floor. 'Where did you get the gryphon feathers?'

'Non! She will kill me,' he screams and spits at me with venom and fury.

His voice shifts to a stronger Arcadian accent as his emotional state visibly turns to one of fear and desperation. 'She thinks she is a so-called red queen, but she's a *taweille*, a witch, you know – a *rouge diablesse*, a red she-devil born of savages. I sold my soul to her and cannot break my contract with her. I will not reveal her whereabouts.'

To my astonishment LeBlanc slithers free from Yoshiko with a burst of inhuman strength and scrambles for his gun on the floor.

'I will never tell you! Never!'

He stands and points the revolver straight at me. But

his hand tremors as he pulls the trigger. The frame of a landscape painting to my left splinters into fragments.

Yoshiko unsheathes her knife with the graceful movement of a huntress. LeBlanc turns to evade her, but stumbles over a discarded absinthe bottle. His forehead hits the oak table with a loud crack and his body flops with a thud onto the floor.

As she lifts his head, dark red lines stream down his forehead and over his face.

'He's dead,' she declares and points towards the table. 'Quickly, fetch his Babbage engine and collect any papers that you think are important. We're leaving.'

As I turn, I see from the corner of my eye Yoshiko brushing LeBlanc's forehead with her left hand. Like a moggy washing its paws, she then licks the ruby stains from her fingertips. I look away in horror and gather what I can fit into a leather satchel. My legs feel like jelly, but I carry on and comb the room looking everywhere for useful scraps of information – everywhere except where there is a growing pool of crimson on the floor.

I descend the stairs for breakfast after another night of awful dreams and find Father quarrelling with Yoshiko.

'Don't worry, I made it look like LeBlanc had committed suicide,' growls Yoshiko.

'Are you sure you covered your tracks, *maulkin*?' retorts father in a brusque manner.

'Yes! And don't ever call me that ever again Warnock-san!'

'And left no clues that would implicate us?'

'Yes,' hisses Yoshiko like an alley cat trapped in a tight corner.

'Well, let us deliberate upon your findings.' Father turns his back on her and stares out the main window into the morning sunshine.

Breakfast is already laid out on the dining table. There are boiled dodo's eggs, baked fur-bearing trout fillets set in jelly, a bowl of rice and sliced lemons.

'Eat your eggs, Alice,' Father barks. 'You know it is good for your undead disposition.' With reluctance I peel off the blue shell and force myself to ingest this bitter tasting delicacy with the help of a slice of lemon.

'I examined the micro-Babbage engine files and read through most of the papers you collected. Apparently there have been numerous payments made to the Palace of Wonderland near Cantonesetown. So many, in fact, that it appears LeBlanc was close to bankruptcy.'

Father stops in a moment of reflection and drags on his pipe. He blows a thick smoke cloud towards us. Yoshiko coughs and chokes on her dish of rice and fish, which she pecks at with chopsticks. She grabs a cup of green tea to clear her throat. I watch father chuckle to himself.

'I am not surprised our Arcadian hatter found himself in a spot of trouble, especially around this part of town. This quarter is controlled by organised underworld gangs and is nothing but an Aladdin's cave of thieves. Judging from his violent behaviour towards to you, my dears, I think he may have smoked too much *Hindoo ganja* or was afflicted by some brain-rotting disease caught from paying for the services of too many *femmes galantes*, no doubt.'

Father grabs a newspaper from the floor at the foot of the chair. He flings it open on the table with a sweep of his metallic arm. 'But see here, we may have an interesting lead with regards to the witch.' He jabs his pipe at a small advertisement with a flamboyant border. 'An illusionist who calls herself the Red Queen performs at the Palace. Perhaps, she may be the *rouge diablesse* who haunted our dearly departed hatter.' Father grabs another newspaper lying on the edge of the table. 'Moreover, this advertisement in the Torontopolis Telegraph states they are looking for women who can sing and dance, and the auditions are fortuitously being held today, 17th of October, 1878.'

Father clamps my shoulder with his heavy brass hand and proclaims, 'You and Yoshiko will pay a visit to Wonderland under the pretence of being show hall girls. Reconnoitre around the building and find this Red Queen.'

'And what if she is not there?' I ask father, while attempting to appear braver than I feel. He releases his brass grip and my shoulder aches with pain.

'Search her dressing room. Turn the theatre upside-down, for all I bloody care. But find me answers that will lead me to the source of the gryphon feathers!'

We catch a horse drawn coach to Cantonesetown for we couldn't afford a ride in the opulent horseless carriages used by the rich. So far, it has been a more pleasurable experience than the steam-powered cart from last night. I find the confined quarters of the small cab comforting. The doors, walls and roof are made of dark wood and smell of pine oil polish. The seats are covered in green upholstery with a velvety softness that is a pleasure to stroke with my fingertips.

In the privacy of the carriage I also feel safe and secure. I gather enough courage to ask the question that has been bothering me since this morning: 'What's a *maul-kin*, Yoshiko?'

She sits silent and still like a statue, but her eyebrows furrow.

'Please, what is it?'

'It's an old word for a cat, but it has other meanings – hag, witch's demon and some other more derogatory ones.'

To my astonishment Yoshiko then does something that I have never seen this fierce lioness of a woman do – she chokes and sobs. One or two tears drop from her eyes like delicate pearls.

'I am tired of being humiliated all the time by Warnock. And tired of his cruel treatment of you, Alice.' She wipes away her tears and turns her head to gaze out the carriage window. 'Sometimes, I think you would have been better off in that vile orphanage run by the Sisters.'

I freeze and blink in disbelief. Had she just said orphanage? But I have always lived with my father for as long as I can remember. It's just frustrating that father won't tell me anything about my mother – for my own good, he always says. However, it is hard to reconcile the fact that there isn't any evidence of her existence within our house. Nothing.

Yoshiko shifts in her seat and stares at me. 'Alice, can't you remember anything before your accident?'

Her tone of voice is warm, and there is no hint of her icy demeanour. Upon hearing this question though, I know she has articulated something I dread to admit to myself – I cannot recall anything from my childhood except for the stuffed toy from my horrible dream. And I almost remember its name – Lord Brian, no, Bryon, I think.

A chorus of whinnies brings me back to reality as the coach clatters to a halt in front of the Palace of Wonderland. The theatre is situated on Kings Street at the edge of Cantonesetown. The backstreets and alleys behind it are full of shops, street stalls, opium dens, illegal gambling saloons and brothels.

The Palace is a massive red brick building based on the architectural design of a neo-gothic revival cathedral. Just past the outdoor ticket booth, hangs a large poster that proclaims:

For One Night Only!
Direct from Faraway Cornish Lands
"The Lobster Quadrille"
Performed by the renowned
Mock Turtle Troupe

Inside the foyer is a wall covered with framed polychrome prints of performers, past and present; they have labels, which help identify the performer in question. Yoshiko waves to me and points to a portrait of a native woman, perhaps Métis, but photographic shadows obscure details of her face. She wears a silk red dress and her head is covered with an oriental turban featuring an upright gryphon feather. Upon the label is printed: "The Red Queen, Fortune-teller, Seeress and Illusionist Extraordinaire."

'Ahem! Ladies, are you here for the audition?' A man in a bright green plaid jacket with a bushy ginger beard steps forward. He puffs a cigar held in a mechanical extension device and speaks with an exaggerated urbanite inflection.

'Yes,' hisses Yoshiko.

'Well then, hurry along. Just go through the main doors into the auditorium.'

I smile and stroll up the steps into the main hall.

I have never seen an empty theatre before. The grandeur of the elaborate architectural decorations and massive glass chandeliers is overwhelming. Everything seems to be draped in soft blue velvet. I feel that I'm lost in a submarine palace of Atlantis.

Yoshiko grabs my hand and ushers me towards a side door near the stage. The ginger bearded man does not follow us and nobody on the stage notices our entrance, as they are too busy rehearsing.

In the backstage area an old stagehand with a creaky iron leg bumps into us.

'Can I help you ladies?' he stammers with a thick maritime accent.

'We are looking for the Red Queen,' demands Yoshiko in a hurried voice.

'So she can read our fortunes,' I add with a nervous laugh.

'Up the stairs, third floor, towards the end of corridor.'

I thank him and we ascend the rickety wooden staircase.

The third floor hallway is long and lit by sombre storm lanterns. The darkness, which clings around the edges, gives the corridor an eerie appearance as if it is an underground lair. The smell of mould saturates the air and I retch. I have never experienced such a physical sensation of uncontrollable disquiet before. I feel as if am falling down a rabbit hole into the bowels of the earth. But Yoshiko steadies me and we move with cautious steps down the passage.

Eventually, we reach a door with a playing card pinned to it – the Queen of Hearts.

Yoshiko raps on the door and it creaks open. The smell of burning sweetgrass permeates the air.

'Come in,' says a woman, but I can't place her accent.

Yoshiko coils and readies herself to spring like a high-strung cheetah. She unsheathes her blade and I follow her inside. I feel queasy in my stomach.

The room is bathed in the soft light of tallow candles and the haze of sweetgrass fumes stings my eyes.

I hear Yoshiko state, 'I had my suspicions, but I know who you are, Red Queen, or should I say …'

Suddenly, something small and soft hits me in the chest. I try to grab it, but it drops to the floor. I lean down and pick up a stuffed white rabbit with buttons for eyes. I recognise it in an instant – the toy from my dreams, Lord Byron!

I have no time to grasp the significance of this new discovery as Yoshiko unleashes a blood-curdling caterwaul that is cut short in mid-scream. The dark form of a tall man stands behind her. His pale right arm clasps her around the waist, while his left hand with long fingernails clamps her mouth shut.

But he is no ordinary human being. He was at least six and half feet tall and his mop of white hair adds at least another five inches to his height. Two small deer antlers sprout from his forehead, while his eyes blaze yellow and glow in the shadows. This is a species of cryptoid that I have never seen before – I'm sure father would know what it is.

Yoshiko stops struggling. A thick frost covers her body and the cryptoid drops her like a rag doll. She hits the floor in an explosion of ice crystals. The bronze coin that hangs around her neck, rolls across the floor and shatters upon hitting the wall.

'Yoshiko!' I cry. 'No, you can't be dead!'

'Be quiet and don't move or my weetigo servant will harm you too, Alice.' The voice comes from a woman with long, dark hair sitting in a chair. She is staring into an oval mirror propped up on a table, but I can't see her face in its reflection.

'How did you know my name?' I gasp.

'I have been watching you, little corpse girl, and the great Professor Euan Warnock, for quite a while now. The professor poses a threat to nature and society alike with his cryptozoological experiments, and I need you to help me.' The Red Queen begins to brush her flowing hair with graceful strokes. 'You see, I called upon a favour from Monsieur LeBlanc and hoped the gryphon feathers would gain Warnock's notice. Louis had a torrid affair with a young actress here at the Palace and bedded her out of wedlock. Like so many rakes, he did not want her once she was with child. In great anguish she ran in front of a horseless carriage and died in hospital. To alleviate his Catholic guilt, I had taken payments to keep this secret quiet and invested them into the upkeep of my theatrical home. But alas, he committed suicide last night – so the newspapers say – and now you are paying me a visit. Coincidence, is it not?'

I feel ashamed of my actions conducted last night in the millinery upon hearing these words.

'I hoped Warnock would have picked up the trail that I laid down for him. I was expecting you and your assassin mistress, but I wished that Warnock could have come along too.'

I edge backwards with slow and careful steps towards the dressing room door. I must get out of here and warn Father!

'Warnock committed horrific acts in the cause of science. And, you, Alice, are living proof of this.'

'Father only seeks to cure my undead disposition,' I retort. 'He brought me back after the accident.' But, as I utter these words, I come to realise that he has never told me what kind of accident.

The Red Queen puts down her brush and begins to braid her hair into two plaits. 'Has Warnock ever mentioned the medical condition of catatonia that simulates a state of death? I doubt it, but it had been documented in a scholarly tome published in Germany a few years ago. Warnock was fascinated by this new discovery and learned the quickest way to render someone into this death-like state was by poison. He also found it easy to purchase unwanted girls from orphanages and sought to condition them. By inducing catatonia through the use of jabberwocky poison, he could destroy memories and reshape the minds of his victims so that they would obey him as if they were his own daughters.'

'My father would have never done such terrible things.' But as I recite these words, I know deep down they are devoid of any credibility. I gasp and clutch my chest. The throbbing scar above my heart could have been a result of the application of a jabberwocky fang by some unpleasant means.

The Red Queen rises from her chair. The smoky atmosphere and dim lighting obscure her face in mist and shadows.

'Alice, my dear Alice, it saddens me to tell you that are not Warnock's daughter. You are the most successful test subject in a long running experiment that has already claimed the lives of several other girls.'

I take another step backward. The door is just within my reach.

'You're not dead, Alice – or should I say Emma. What he has done to you and the other girls is against the will of the Great Creator. I'm an Ojibway medicine woman, what white people would call a witch or seeress. And I want to help heal you with good medicine, while stopping Warnock from playing with bad medicine that he doesn't fully understand.'

I twirl and make a mad dash for the door. The Red Queen snaps her fingers and the weetigo blocks my exit. He grabs me with his hoarfrost hands that are so cold they pass through my garments and sting my skin. I cling onto Lord Byron as the weetigo hauls me like a sack of potatoes to another room. He flings me into a wooden chair and straps my wrists and ankles to the arms and legs with surprising care. My heart beats wildly with fear. Lord Byron lies in a heap by my feet.

The Red Queen appears out of the shadows carrying her mirror. She holds up the looking glass and positions it about two inches before my face. A small patch of mist spreads over the silver surface with my every breath.

'You see – a rotting corpse can't do this.'

She steps back with the mirror and I behold the pale face of a girl with mismatched eyes and ghastly skin. I see the vapour of my breath disappear from the surface of the glass. My visage contorts from the contraction of my facial muscles and my mouth opens wide. I can no longer contain my vast and cavernous despair – I break down and cry with deep, heavy sobs that shake my entire body and rattle the chair.

After an eternity, I feel the heavy weight of lethargy dragging me deep into the realms of slumber.

I scream and wake from yet another sleep full of nightmares.

I feel a strange tightness at my wrists and look down to see ropes strapping me to the chair. The sun shines from a far window into what appears to be a large storeroom full of

curtains and fabrics. Above me is an ornate metal fixture on the ceiling that I recognise.

During my extensive training programme, over the past couple of years, I have learnt many useful skills. And escaping from tight bonds is one of them. I free my hands with great ease and kneel over to untie my aching ankles.

I move the chair under the chandelier. A metal curtain rod lies on the floor below the window and I remove its white curtain. Standing on the chair, I strike the chandelier with a hard blow. After several knocks, it falls with a clatter to the floor. A broken gas pipe dangles from the ceiling. I jump down and remove the mechanical igniter from inside its frame.

I dash to the gas switch by the door. With one flick the gas flow turns on. A soft hiss fills the room.

I drape myself in the white curtain, which feels coarse and itchy. I pick up Lord Byron and embrace him. After a night of a thousand tears, I surprise myself in having enough water left in my body for them to roll down my cheeks again.

I cup my hands on the door and scream, 'Help me. Please, someone help meeee!'

A few moments later there is a click of the lock. I position myself with my back near to the window.

The door is flung open and the weetigo lumbers in, wheezing cold vapours from his mouth and nostrils. The Red Queen strides to the centre of the room. In the daylight I see a long scar stretching across the left side of her face. But it is her eyes that startle me the most – they are mismatched like mine, and tinted brown and blue.

'Emma, I see you are awake. How are you enjoying your new breath of life?'

I stare at her with a vehement gaze and cry, 'You don't understand. I enjoy being a walking corpse!'

A smile spreads across the Red Queen's face; but is it one of sympathy or indifference?

'I don't want to know about the terrible things that occurred in my previous life. I'm clever enough to understand that if I learn any more details, they will only drown me in a sea of despair. I was blissful in thinking that I was undead, and loved my training as an apprentice thief. But I can't cope any longer – it all has to come to an end.' I lift up the mechanical igniter for her to see.

The Red Queen's eyebrows knit in bewilderment, but then she tilts her head and hears the hissing. She looks upward and finds the damage I have made to the ceiling. Her face becomes a visage of astonishment and alarm.

I give Lord Byron a tight squeeze and strike the flintlock. Once …

… twice …

… and after the third time sparks jump forth. The igniter's nozzle flickers into flame and I hurl the device at the Red Queen.

I fling the window open and leap out as a great explosion shakes the room.

The hungry blaze of the unstoppable inferno continues to devour the entire theatre for hours until it is razed to the ground.

FANTASY

SNOW WHITE

By Sally Mitcham

Shattered ghosts serenade me now. Half-felt fingers pluck at my clothes and, as they whisper that endless mournful song, their cold breath stirs my hair. As I sit here I know She is there with them, just beyond my vision, her eyes pleading those unanswerable questions: Why me? What did I do? But if I turn she will retreat into the shadows with all the rest. You may mock and say these are the creations of a fevered imagination; that the breath is just a breeze from the open window, and the sound nought but the summer wind stirring the trees. But I know what I know. Often, I wake from snowy dreams to the memory of her crying out or find a still-damp footprint on the stair.

Perhaps it is the punishment of a guilty conscience, but I wouldn't do anything differently; would not change one single thing. I'm not ashamed to admit that I'd rather live every day with her haunting than have another hour eaten away by the jealousy I felt whilst she still lived.

The girl stood at her window looking out onto a new white world. She didn't know what had woken her. All was quiet but, rather than return to the warmth of her blankets, she remained to gaze out on this fairie scene. A silver birch pranced in a delicate lace dress and the larch wept whitely. Each leaf on the holly had been dusted with frosting and drifts of snow banked up against the stone sundial. Familiar sights muffled and disguised by the blanket of winter.

She rested her forehead against the window, her eye

drawn to three dark sticks in the shape of an arrow on the pristine snow below. No footsteps led to or from them. Yet there the arrow was, calling to her, urging her towards the woods.

She threw a shawl over her nightgown and whispered down the stairs on slippered feet to ease back the door bolt. The household slumbered on, unaware of her fate.

Except for me.

I heard her leave and knew my careful planning had served me well. My magic was learnt from the nurse who dandled me on her knee and cared for me more than my mother ever had. When She came along, an old nurse wasn't good enough and my protector was discarded to live in poverty on the outskirts of the village. I still visited her, sneaking out to her cottage whenever I could escape from my lessons and chores. As I turned onto her path, she would always be waiting for me, door open, shawl clutched around her stooped shoulders and showing her crooked teeth in a welcoming grin. 'There you are then, my cherub,' she would say as she chivvied me inside to the meagre fireplace and pressed a cup of milk into my hands.

The village children would laugh at her and throw stones when she wasn't looking. But I watched those who did come: pale women who clutched guiltily at their bellies and left even paler; young men who would lose their swagger as they ventured up the path, only to pick it up again as they left; and tired old folk who came away with a youthful step. And all the while I learnt. I learnt what herbs to pick in the dark woods and which to let alone. I learnt the ancient words to say as they were chopped and mixed and stirred. I learnt how to quicken a babe in the womb, and how to end one, how to cure ills and how to cause them. And I learnt the darker arts too.

'... I cannot live without her, I tell you.'

'Come, come, my lord. Was it not just a sennight past that you were crying undying love for the other girl. What is it they call her?'

'I care no more for her now than the rats in the dungeon care for gold and fine silks. No, my Blanche is the only woman I can ever love.'

'And what of her parentage and status?'

'Parentage be damned. You have only to look on that face to know she is born of angels ...'

'Angels, hmmm? Can't argue with that.'

'What was that? Speak up, man! Stop muttering!'

'Twas nothing, my lord. Nothing at all. If you would care to look over these papers now?'

He was mine. Had been courting me for months with his fine words and even finer gifts. But then She returned and he no longer saw me. I was there when they first met. He had come to take me riding, but as I came down the stairs towards him his smile died and was replaced by a gawp of witless wonder. I had no need to turn to see his vision. She was dressed in white as was her habit, dark hair tumbling to her waist and that smile hovering just behind her perfect lips. When an angel appears, men no longer see mortals. Against her charms, I had no chance.

She stole him from me, just as she had stolen everything – from my hobby horse to my father's love. But I vowed that she would never enjoy her latest toy.

Her steps took her past sundial and friendly birch, through wrought-iron gates and into the silence of the watching wood. Her black velvet slippers were soon soaked through and her hair dusted with snow from drooping branches, but the cold never touched her.

Onwards the arrows led her to the deep heart of the

wood and an ancient clearing. There she was stopped by the sight of a plinth carved in crystal-clear ice on which rested an apple. In a monochrome world of bare-branch black and snow white, excepting only her crimson shawl, the apple sang out in splendid reds and greens. Its perfect curves and lustrous skin invited the bite; mesmerised by its beauty, she reached out for it.

One bite. One cry. And she fell.

'Send to the stable to saddle my grey mare at once.'

'But my lord, 'tis past one. Surely this can wait till the morning?'

'I tell you, I dreamt of her. She is in the utmost danger. She falls ...'

'A nightmare, my lord, that is all. You should wait till the morrow, and then ride to see her in a more seemly fashion. Imagine what people will say.'

'Blanche needs me. No more arguments, man. Do as I say!'

I heard them first. In the icy silence of winter all sounds are magnified. The hallooing of those with him, the snorting breath of horses pushed hard, hooves cutting the icy crust and the jangle of harnesses. But he was too late to hear her last cry, see her fall. That was my pleasure alone.

She lay there, arms flung out in sensual abandon, dark locks spread on the snow, her shawl a spreading bloodstain beneath her.

'Over here!' he cried, reining the horse hard in a flurry of snowflakes. Jumping down, he gathered her up in his arms and kissed her cold lips. The arms that should have held me tight. The kisses that belonged to me. And, as I watched the final blossoming of my plan, pleasure turned to bitter ashes in my stomach.

He never returned to me. I crept back to the house

to be safe in my bed before they came thundering to the entrance, crying 'Murder'. I joined in the weeping and wailing, gnashing of teeth and vows of revenge. I was never suspected and hardly even noticed. In death, as in life, she eclipsed me.

My father shut up the house, and now spurns all visitors. No-one comes courting now, but I have my little pleasures. And my ghosts. Do you laugh at me now, sister dear? Think that you won in the end? Well, I care not. He may not have come back to me, but you lost him too.

THE FINAL RECKONING

By Sam Payter

In the half-light of dusk the cliff rose, craggy, sheer, looking insurmountable. They lurked in the shadows at its base, those chosen to climb throwing nervous glances at the punishing granite rock face before them.

Hadaran stood apart from his men, peering through the gloom trying to see a safe path.

The warlock Taldaran, his brother, moved to stand by him. With a chuckle the tall man said, 'There is a reason they fear no attack from this side.' He looked up at the cliff. 'Suicide!'

Hadaran glanced at the warlock, and pointed at the giant eagle totem emblazoned on his chest. 'We can't all fly!' he said gruffly. The warlock laughed before returning to the prince.

Out of the gloom, a rope tumbled down the cliff. Lost in the shadows above, Hadaran knew that Thendril, the elf sent by the Elven-King to aid Prince Akbar, was already scaling the forbidding rocks. It was time. 'To me, men,' he ordered.

'Yes General,' came the unenthusiastic response.

A fighting general, Hadaran always led from the front, so he stepped forward, gripped the rope and began to haul his massive frame up the cliff.

Soon the ground below was lost in the gloom. Hadaran could hear the prince shouting encouragement, and knew that it irked him not be with his men. Prince Akbar was still a boy to Hadaran's seasoned eyes, despite the fifteen years of warfare they had seen together. Hadaran respected Akbar's father and knew that he had been a good king, but he cursed the old man every day for not having ratified his heir with the Assembly of Ministers, and blamed him for the fifteen years of bloody, treacherous fighting that had followed. The king's only daughter, and eldest son, had died in the conflict, the son by Hadaran's own hand. As he reached for another handhold, he navigated a small shrub clinging desperately to the rock. He could hear the exertions of the men around him and longed to reach the summit, but all he could see was unforgiving rock.

Gradually the prince's voice faded away as they climbed further and the rest of the ground party moved into position. One hand forward, one foot forward, inch by inch Hadaran continued. He looked up and saw Thendril securing the lead rope in place before easing further up the tortuous slope. Hadaran's arms began to tremble and he paused, as men strained above and below. Suddenly the soldier above lost his footing, and a shower of dirt rained down seconds before the man slid down the rock face. As he passed, Hadaran thrust out his left arm and used all of his considerable strength to grab and hold him against the rock. He could feel his own footholds loosening with the added weight. 'Find a handhold!' he gasped through gritted teeth.

The soldier scrambled around for a few terrified seconds before the weight on Hadaran's arm was removed. Once sure of his footing the soldier looked at his general, gratitude replacing panic in his eyes. 'Thank you, sir.'

'On your way,' Hadaran responded. The man began to scramble upwards and, despite the distinguishing scar running from cheek to chin, Hadaran realised he did not know his name. At the start of the war, then a major, he had known the name of each man under his command but, after fifteen long hard years of fighting, so many of those names were gone, replaced by new ones, not expected to last long enough to require the need to be learnt. *How many will survive this desperate gamble, and what horrors await them at the summit?* Fearing the answer, he continued the interminable climb.

As the two moons reached their apex, Hadaran hauled himself onto a ledge below the imposing brick walls of Katrang, the city perched at the top of the cliff.

Thendril motioned for quiet, as now the danger of discovery was all too real. Gradually, the men all gained the ledge and there rested before ascending the city walls. Close to the top the elf signalled silence. Above, Hadaran heard footsteps and then voices.

'Ah, the boredom!' complained a soldier of the Citadel Guards.

'Boredom is good,' replied another. 'Boredom means you're safe. You young ones want to see action, but action means you end up dead.'

'So you've seen plenty of action?'

'Aye, before I joined the Guards, I was there from the start with General Dathkar.'

Hadaran's heart pulsed faster at the mention of that name.

'You were at the sacking of Ithilia?' asked the veteran's companion.

'Aye, one minute we was guarding the city in the name of Prince Akbar, the next Dathkar declared himself a general and ordered the city sacked. Umm, a bloody day that one. Not soldiering that. That was plain murder - women, children ...'

Hadaran's stomach clenched as nausea swept over him; the faces of his wife and child, killed by his one-time friend Dathkar amidst the slaughter of that day, flashed before him. His self-control waivered, then crumbled. He drew his sword, intent on gutting the guard above, the importance of the mission forgotten in the torment of memory. But, before he could act, Thendril leapt over the parapet with inhuman power and speed and killed both guards before either could cry out. He hauled the rest of the party over before hiding the bodies. A quick glance from the elf was all the admonishment Hadaran needed and he cursed himself for his lack of control. His thirst for vengeance had driven him through all the years of hardship, waiting for the one chance to face Dathkar, but he knew what they attempted now meant more. This was their only chance to finish the war, to finally kill Rok and place Akbar on the throne, and he had nearly jeopardised that. Taking a deep breath he nodded to Thendril, who ghosted away towards the service gate.

They reached the gate undetected but now Hadaran could see no way to stealthily remove the guards. They were too many and too spread out. He looked at the elf, who simply drew his slender sword, placed it at his feet and then strung his longbow while the rest of the men readied themselves. As soon as the first guard fell from an arrow, Hadaran charged, shouting his infamous war cry, 'To the death!'

The soldiers of Prince Rok's mercenary army feared those words more than any other, and the unexpectedness of hearing them inside the walls of their capital meant that many were slaughtered before they could even draw their swords, but a sergeant rallied the remaining guards before rushing to ring the alarm bell. Hadaran knew that if he succeeded, they were doomed. An arrow from Thendril took another guard who had unwittingly stepped in front of the sergeant. Hadaran drew his war axe and, with deadly precision, cut a path through to the sergeant before he reached the alarm bell. Skidding to a halt, the terrified sergeant stared at the blood-spattered axe as Hadaran asked, 'Were you at Ithilia?'

Confused by the question, the sergeant nodded. Confusion became terror as Hadaran leapt in the air and swung his axe to deal a crushing blow, biting into the man's shoulder and continuing to his midriff. The remaining guards watched in horror and quickly threw down their weapons in surrender. Hadaran's men paused and looked to their general. Knowing they could take no prisoners, he shook his head and watched as the men were put to the sword. The harshness of the war had numbed Hadaran to killing and death, but the condemned men's screams momentarily caused him to turn away until the word Ithilia and the image of his wife's face flashed through his brain, as it had done on countless occasions, and the revulsion left him.

'Open the gates for the prince!' he ordered.

The prince entered the city and Hadaran took note of how he moved through the blood and guts with barely a flicker of emotion. *The war has changed us all*, he thought sadly.

The prince's steely grey eyes burned with determination as he whispered, 'Now we finish this.'

Shadows crept over the rough, cobbled streets in the poor district of Katrang. Hundreds of leagues from the front line, the grand city claimed by Prince Rok as his capital, had suffered little in the war, its population ignorant to the carnage and brutality raging through the lands of Dakabar. That was all about to change.

Prince Akbar's small, highly skilled band stalked through the cramped and littered streets, flitting from one shadow to another, silently making their way to the citadel at the heart of the city. Suddenly the silence and gloom were broken. A man emerged from a well-lit room onto the street. Hadaran held his breath as all his men froze in place, but to no avail. The ignorant citizen walked straight into two soldiers, who reacted with deadly quickness, anticipating their general's orders. The body slumped to the floor amidst a pile of rubbish.

Another victim. Hadaran spared a brief thought for the unlucky soul and watched as the prince hurried past at a crouch, not even acknowledging the man who had just been murdered in his name. *Fifteen years ago, he would have stood in mute horror staring at the corpse, but not anymore.*

As a young general, Akbar had sided   with his eldest brother Obridan, believing him to be the rightful heir. Now, that young general was long gone, pity and compassion driven from him by bloodshed and treachery. The mere act of choosing a side, standing with one sibling against the rest had caused him no end of turmoil, but he had done what he had believed to be right.

Hadaran remembered standing there watching the young man as he was driven to his knees with grief on learning that his youngest brother, Rok, had betrayed and killed his beloved sister. Akbar had then discovered that Obridan had grown fearful of his power and enlisted the powerful warlock, Talderan, to kill him; only, Talderan's loyalty to Hadaran had led him to reveal the betrayal.

And so began the bitterest chapter of the war as Akbar and Obridan fought a bloody campaign, former friends and allies slaughtering each other in great numbers, before Obridan's forces were finally defeated. Hadaran had observed the young prince's turmoil, as he had ordered his brother beheaded. The last of the Prince's innocence and compassion had fled that day.

And what of me? When did compassion leave me? Hadaran thought to himself as, with a simple flick of his hand, another citizen of Katrang was killed. Ithilia; that same grim day that had witnessed the death of Obridan had become a day of despair for Hadaran. As reports of Dathkar's betrayal and the sacking of the city reached them, Hadaran had marched his army remorselessly back to the capital, desperate to save his wife and child, but it had been a futile gesture. Hadaran and his men had known they were too late when they reached the city and saw the smoke billowing from it. The opportunity for grief had been short lived as Prince Rok's army appeared to receive the city from Dathkar, only to be set upon by the enraged army of Hadaran. The fury with which they had fought had decimated their enemy, forcing Rok and Dathkar to flee with the shattered remnants of the armies, all the way to the safety of Katrang. *But it is safe no more!*

Hadaran could see the citadel now, looming above the city in the pre-dawn gloom.

Thendril ghosted out of the shadows. 'We are nearing the citadel, but the population begins to stir. If we do not attack soon, there will be a bloodbath.'

Hadaran could sense the eagerness of the men around him, those who had lost loved ones in Ithilia. He knew they wanted that bloodbath, craved that slaughter, and knew that he shared their feelings. He looked at Prince Akbar, half in anticipation, half in trepidation, but the prince shook his head firmly. A moment of regret passed over Hadaran, yet he knew the Prince was right. The sacking of Ithilia was a heinous act and Akbar was better than that. Hadaran saw a brief glimmer of relief cross the face of Thendril, before noting concern on the elf's usually composed features.

'What is it?' he asked.

'There are dark forces at work around the citadel. I do not understand their nature but I fear their touch.'

Hadaran looked to Talderan who said with grimness in his voice, 'Klashva.'

A murmur of fear rose up from the soldiers at the mention of that name. Rok's warlock and his feared golden dragon totem had caused the death of hundreds of Hadaran's men and brought many a decisive victory for Rok's mercenary army. Klashva had sided the Council of Magic with Prince

Rok, and many had followed him. Talderan and those magi loyal to him had joined Akbar, and had managed to destroy all but Klashva and those closest to him.

The tall warlock beckoned his magi forward as he said to Akbar and Hadaran, 'This is a battle many years in the making.' He looked Hadaran in the eye. 'Your force cannot contend with Klashva. Destroy Rok's Citadel Guard and kill as many of the magi as you can, but leave Klashva to me.'

Hadaran gripped his brother's shoulder and squeezed before watching him leave, hoping he would not become another face haunting his memories. He turned to his men. 'We shall divide our forces. Prince Akbar, you will lead a diversionary assault on the main gate, while Thendril and I capture the postern gate. Once inside the bailey we will take the main gate and then assault the keep together …'

Before he could finish, a deafening roar of thunder and a bright flash of lightning exploded all around the citadel. The pre-dawn gloom was eviscerated as the sky lit up in an array of colours.

'I think they know we are here, lads!' Hadaran shouted, smiling grimly. 'Forward now!' As one, the men raced through the streets, Hadaran following Thendril to the postern gate. They were met by four magi sent by Talderan, all in shock and dishevelled.

One steadied himself enough to explain. 'We set off magical wards protecting the citadel. Had it not been for Talderan we would all be dead. Klashva had set a flame wall to attack us, but he managed to thwart it.'

'Can you get us through that?' Hadaran asked, indicating the thick postern gate, which was heavily guarded.

The mage nodded and uttered words of power, joined by the other three. Though not as powerful as warlocks, magi still possessed the Gift of the Gods and, when joining powers, they could create devastating magic.

Hadaran felt the hairs on his arms and neck raise as they

chanted. Gradually, a small glowing ball of furious white light emerged and began to grow. An alarmed shout from the postern gate told that they had been spotted. Hadaran called for shields to protect the magi, while Thendril picked off the bowmen on the walls.

'Down!' The soldiers bearing shields dropped as the incandescent ball of light sped over their heads and crashed into the postern gate, incinerating it and a large section of the barbican. Stones larger than a man's torso were obliterated in seconds.

Hadaran looked at the exhausted magi in shock as one said sheepishly, 'I fear we may have been a little over zealous! We shall join you shortly.'

Hadaran nodded and charged over the rubble, into the outer bailey. Rok's soldiers were swarming around the citadel, confusion breeding chaos. Hadaran knew he had only a small window of opportunity to reach the main gate and storm the barbican. 'With me men!' he shouted as he raced toward the main gate.

Thendril pointed to a formation of Citadel Guards forming in the bailey before the main gate. Along the walls to either side, magi were engaged in mystical battle; bolts of lightning and balls of flame clashed and sparked, setting the air alive with energy.

Hadaran ordered a squad to clear the walls before charging in behind the Citadel Guards. The element of surprise worked in his favour as they quickly destroyed the ceremonial soldiers; those who survived the onslaught retreated back into the keep, lowering the portcullis and barring the massive gate. Hadaran studied the impenetrable looking keep while the main gate was opened and the prince's force entered the bailey.

Talderan came to stand by his brother before muttering, 'He must have more forces,' giving voice to Hadaran's thoughts.

Suddenly a group of soldiers and magi charged from their left. Talderan reacted instantly, speaking the Words and unleashed a sheet of marching, red-hot flame that decimated the front rank of the attackers. Rok's remaining magi responded with a wave of destructive spells, only to be easily countered by a shield spell cast by Talderan. With a flick of his wrist he caused the spells to rebound off his shield and sent them crashing back into the now terrified magi. Whilst the battle raged the Citadel Guard, bolstered by Rok's King's Guard, charged forward in great numbers. Akbar and Hadaran met the charge with swords drawn.

The general's world constricted. The sounds and vivid illuminations of the battle dimming as he parried a sword thrust from a guard before shoving him onto the point of another's sword, then deftly spun and slashed at the defenceless man, cutting deep into his neck. The red blood fountained into the air, flashing with supernatural patterns as the magi's spells erupted around them, while Hadaran turned to find his next victim. Seeing none, he beheld the carnage around him and knew from years of experience that his force would emerge victorious. However, his triumphant cry died in his throat as a great roar shook the very foundations of the citadel. Hadaran felt true fear for the first time since seeing the smoke rising from Ithilia, as he beheld a mighty golden dragon ascending into the sky above the keep. Its shadow, with wings outstretched, covered the entire bailey. The rising sun caught the golden scales, causing a shimmering light that transfixed the eye.

'It's Klashva!' shouted Talderan, and rapidly incanted words of power.

Hadaran looked up as the dragon stopped its ascent and, with an earth-shattering roar, dived headlong toward Akbar. 'Protect the prince!' he ordered. Five of his men pushed Akbar to the floor and showed their heroism by standing to face the onrushing dragon. A burst of ice-blue flame incinerated them where they stood, but the prince was shielded as the dragon swept overhead, ineffectual arrows and spells bouncing off its scales. Hadaran, knowing they were powerless against it, turned to Talderan, his eyes pleading, but the warlock was crouched to the floor, muttering to himself.

Suddenly a blinding white flash erupted around him and a giant blue eagle soared into the air, screeching its challenge to the golden dragon, whose answering cry was terrifying. The totems of the two most powerful warlocks in Dakabar rose high into the air and circled each other. The dragon belied its almighty size and darted forward, unleashing a burst of flame to engulf the soaring eagle. The fighting below ceased as men on both sides stood mesmerised, watching the titanic struggle. The giant eagle wrapped its wings around itself, its feathers seemingly transforming to become steel. The flames washed over it but it emerged from them, impervious, screeching defiantly. The dragon thundered its rage and bore down on the smaller creature, massive talons primed to crush the bird in mid-air. But Talderan's eagle veered away, allowing the dragon to pass before rising and then diving toward its foe. The golden dragon made the mistake of turning its head toward the onrushing eagle, which tore away at one of its eyes with its talons before deftly moving away. The beast shrieked with pain and rage; half blinded, it bellowed flames in all directions. The eagle glided above, awaiting its opportunity to strike, then swooped and clawed the other eye. In panic, the great dragon lashed out with its tail and swatted the eagle aside, crippling one of its wings. The majestic bird retreated, struggling to gain height because of the injury and yet, up and up it soared until lost from sight.

Hadaran feared for his brother, who was now vulnerable to attack, despite the dragon being blinded. In a frantic maddened rage, the creature tore across the sky, turning this way and that. It lashed out with its tail and struck a corner tower of the keep, reducing it to rubble. Hadaran shouted warning as the masonry tumbled from the sky and crashed down amongst the men standing in the bailey. Many of the Citadel Guard were crushed along with a large number of Rok's magi.

'Look!' shouted Thendril, his finger pointing high into the sky.

Hadaran looked up and saw a blue flame descending from the heavens; it was the giant eagle, plummeting toward the stricken dragon. Seeing what was coming, he called, 'Fall back to the main gate!'

As men scattered from the keep, the giant eagle descended, screeching in triumph as it drew closer. Although blinded, the dragon could still hear, and its head snapped round to the sound, as its great wings pushed it toward the eagle. As the two totems flew at each other, the giant eagle flared its wings and exposed its talons, while the blinded dragon snapped at thin air, unaware of its impending doom. The eagle's talons struck the onrushing dragon and the two plunged downward towards the keep. At the last second the eagle released its grip and veered away. The dragon had no time to halt its trajectory and hurtled into the keep, smashing against it with a thunderous impact, rendering stone and iron alike. The western corner of the keep disappeared in a shower of rubble and dust leaving the vanquished dragon lying broken upon the stones.

Hadaran knew this was his opportunity. From the safety of the main gate he charged forward, followed by the prince and his men, and beset the remaining shell shocked guards, whose resistance had been broken by the felling of the mighty golden dragon. Soon Hadaran stood on the destroyed portcullis, ready to enter the keep and finish the war.

'Keep pushing!' Hadaran growled, his blood racing. Frustration, pain, vengeance, sorrow - all these constant companions followed with him as he and the soldiers hacked their way through the keep towards the Grand Hall. The mercenary soldiers were throwing themselves onto their swords when they should have been surrendering and calling for terms. Confused, Hadaran turned to Talderan, who was protecting Prince Akbar. 'Why do they fight so?' he demanded, his disgust at the killing in front of him, and from all the years past, clearly showing on his face.

'Their eyes!' Talderan responded, pointing to the soldiers engaged before them, eyes blood red and mad. 'They are possessed, they must be under Klashva's spell!'

'But he is dead; you destroyed him!' Akbar shouted, the frustration telling in his voice.

'His holding spells will linger till his spirit is taken by the gods. He must still be alive. Hadaran, come with me.'

'Keep pushing forward. Cut them down if you have to!' the general ordered reluctantly, before following the warlock into the decimated quarter of the keep.

Picking their way through the rubble, they found the crushed and broken body of Klashva. His legs and arms were twisted at grotesque angles and his cracked and jagged ribs jutted from his chest; yet his breath still rattled from between his smashed teeth. Bloody, scarred eye sockets stared vacantly ahead but he seemed to sense their approach. He tried to raise his mangled fingers but failed.

'By all the Gods,' whispered Hadaran, 'he still lives.'

'His spirit clings to life,' Talderan said. 'Finish him. Take his head.'

Hadaran nodded, drew his axe and loomed over the prone, crushed figure, and slashed down to sever the head.

'Is it done?' Hadaran asked hopefully.

Talderan looked worried. 'He may have cast spells using

necromancy that will endure even after his death. We have not won the day yet.'

They turned and hurried back to the Grand Hall to find a group of mercenaries being held as prisoners, eyes no longer mad but instead looking dazed and confused.

Hadaran turned to his captain, who reported the events. 'They suddenly stopped fighting. When a few were cut down they all surrendered. The Grand Hall has been barred from within.' The captain paused, eyeing his general warily. 'They say Dathkar is in there, preparing a last defence.'

Hadaran could feel the men's gaze on him, knew that they could feel his thirst for vengeance; saw fear in their eyes, fear of a man they loved, of what he would do to sate that thirst. He gripped his axe, all sorrow and regret gone, ready to release his fury. He turned to Talderan and, indicating the huge wooden doors that barred their entrance to the Grand Hall, said quietly, 'Take them down.'

The warlock stared into Hadaran's eyes and had to look away from what he saw there. He knew that death was coming to all those inside, death in the form of his brother, and nothing could save them. He gathered his power, spoke the Words and the giant doors that had stood for hundreds of years disintegrated in a shower of splinters. Inside the Hall, men lay strewn from the force of the explosion. As the dust settled they could see Rok, cowering on a throne. Before him stood a giant of a man, his great hairy beard failing to hide the look of shock on his face.

'Dathkar!' Hadaran screamed, years of rage and pain unleashed.

The giant man quickly recovered and barked orders; soldiers of the King's Guard flooded the doorway, but all were scythed down by the enraged general. *Not with a thousand men could they stop him*, Talderan thought sadly as he watched his brother lose himself to bloodlust. Akbar ordered his men forward and the King's Guard were quickly destroyed.

Hadaran leaned on his axe, panting, oblivious to the death and carnage around him. He saw Rok furtively seeking an escape route, snapping at Dathkar to act. He met the eyes of his enemy, unsure of what he wanted to see in them. *Fear, guilt?* But what he saw was simply resignation, a man who knew he was about to die.

Dathkar turned from that stare to face Akbar, as he laid his sword on the ground and knelt, head bowed, before pleading in a low voice, 'Your Majesty, I place myself at your mercy.'

Akbar was momentarily confused by the gesture. His grim determination began to waver. Hadaran, seeing this, gripped his axe and waited, coiled, ready to unleash the violence he craved now, yet battling to control it should his prince grant Dathkar his life.

Dathkar could not help but look at his foe once more. 'I did not mean for them to die,' he whispered regretfully, so only Hadaran could hear. It was too much; his wife's loving smile and his child's innocent eyes appeared in his mind and all control was gone.

He screamed with rage, then spun, swung his axe and buried it deep into Dathkar's skull, denying him the soldier's honour of a clean death. The axe slid from his hand as the giant corpse twitched and toppled slowly to the floor, graphically symbolising the central pillar of Hadaran's existence since Ithilia, his vengeance, crumbling within him. He sank to his knees and sobbed as the pain of his lost family finally engulfed him.

'Brother, please, please, come closer. Embrace me, brother!' Rok began whimpering from behind his throne, his eyes mad.

Akbar stepped forward to face him and met his gaze with cold grey eyes. 'You are no brother of mine. This ends now.'

Rok laughed maniacally. 'You are right - finally I have you.'

Hadaran's sobbing ceased, and his head rose, sensing something was awry, his woe banished, locked inside of him again, as all that he had left - his duty - returned.

Rok continued. 'Klashva created a spell to protect me,' he said, stepping forward and drawing his ceremonial sword, swaying and stumbling like a drunkard, his golden robes rustling with each oncoming step.

'Hadaran!' Talderan shouted in warning.

Hadaran rose sharply, struggling to understand Rok's words but hearing the alarm in Talderan's voice. 'Protect the King!' he shouted, as soldiers rushed forward and launched attacks on Rok, who stood, arms splayed wide as the swords bounced and deflected from him, before cutting down those nearest to him and advancing on Akbar.

Talderan blasted him with a sheet of flame but Rok just laughed. 'No magic can harm me, warlock! Klashva's spell! Yes, many died! Yes, yes, many died so that I may live!'

Soldiers continued to throw themselves at him but no blade could touch him.

He laughed. 'No mystic power or man-made blade can harm me!'

Hadaran recognised the danger and began pushing Akbar out of the Hall. 'We cannot protect you. You must flee.'

'We are so close, so close to finishing it!' Akbar seethed, though his fear was evident as Rok cut down two more soldiers and bore down on them.

Hadaran shoved the prince away and turned to face Rok, ready to give his life, just as Thendril appeared by his side, and handed him a small dagger.

'Made by my people,' he said.

Hadaran smiled grimly and faced Rok, who laughed even harder as Hadaran brandished the blade, not seeing the danger in his madness. The general ducked a wild swing and charged forward before ramming the dagger into Rok's chest. The air exploded from the mad Prince's lungs, crazed eyes now stunned as he sank to his knees and coughed up blood.

'How?' he asked weakly.

Hadaran gripped his hair and pulled his head back, holding the dagger before his eyes. 'Not man-made; elven-made, you bastard!' He looked at Akbar, saw pain, rage and sadness on his face before giving a nod of the head and closing his eyes, shutting in the regret.

Hadaran turned his attention once more to Rok's pleading, desperate, mad eyes. *Just one more life, one more death and it is over …* And yet, his hand would not move; the hand that had killed a hundred men, but could not kill one more. Again, the loving smile and innocent eyes of his family came to his mind, but this time there was no rage, no anger, only sadness. Immersed in sorrow he barely noticed the dagger being taken from his hand.

'Broth-' Rok didn't finish his plea as Akbar thrust the dagger into his throat and ripped across, a spray of blood splattering both their faces.

Hadaran could not believe his eyes. The boy prince, all innocence and joy, was gone for good. Before him now stood a man, driven, determined … ruthless. *Now you are a King,* his eyes spoke when they met Akbar's. Grim silence was his reply, but behind it were glimpses of sorrow and relief. The good prince was still there, still in need of protection. Hadaran shut his grief away, deep inside himself, the empty space within him vacated by vengeance now filling with a sense of duty to his king.

'The war is won!' he shouted, and all those in the hall cheered, except Akbar who stood staring at his brother's corpse, the chants of "All hail the king!" lost on him.

Finally he looked at Hadaran with tears in his eyes as his

general knelt and said softly, 'King Akbar, lord of Dakabar. All hail the king!'

WHERE THE OCEAN
MEETS THE SKY

By Barbara Stevenson

'Pull her hard to starboard,' the mate called.

'Hard to starboard,' the hand said.

'We'll crash into the rocks, sir.' The midshipman grabbed the wheel.

'Captain's orders, hard to starboard,' the mate said.

'That's not hard to starboard,' the midshipman said. 'It's quarter to nine.'

The mate turned to look at the captain. The hands on the tall, wooden grandfather clock that was propped against the main mast, lashed to it with ropes, showed the time was fifteen minutes to nine. On cue it croaked out the first three lines of the Westminster chime.

'As you were, sailor,' the mate said, swinging his arms behind his back to twiddle with his thumbs. The ship scraped past the outcrop of rocks. 'What course are we on?'

'You don't know?' The midshipman's voice sounded like a tomcat hissing, which didn't surprise the mate. The midshipman had ginger fur, ten centimetre long whiskers and a battle scar on his striped tail.

'How should I know? I only boarded ten minutes ago,' the mate said. 'I was starching my beard ready for our passing out parade when I got the message that your ship was short-staffed.'

'Not so bad that we need a naval college moron to guide us,' the midshipman said.

'Watch your tongue, sir. I could have you court-martialled

for insub … insubor … cheek.'

The midshipman ran his tongue over his left hand and washed behind his ear.

'Don't do that when I'm addressing you,' the mate said. 'Where are the rest of the crew?'

'There's just you, me, the hand and Captain Clock,' Midshipman Tom said. 'But you can hardly ask the captain to chip in with the men.'

At that the ship's hand burst into a fit of giggles.

Tom groaned. 'We'll be late for the Infanta's tennis tournament now.'

The hand was rolling so hard on the deck that the ship listed. The mate was caught off balance and stumbled towards the midshipman. Tom leapt aside as the mate - all six-foot-two and fourteen stone of him - crashed into the grandfather clock. The wood creaked and the hour hand slipped to dangle over the six.

'I'm terribly sorry, Captain.' The mate saluted.

'Roc ahoy,' Tom said.

'Steer round it,' the mate said.

'It's a roc, not a rock,' Tom clarified.

'It can't be. They only exist in poems and picture books,' the mate said.

'Ordinarily yes, sir,' Tom agreed, 'but they will leave the pages, if there is something worth dying for.'

'Nothing is worth dying for.' The mate ducked as the huge bird cruised over his head.

'We've got nothing on board,' Tom said. 'We did have a present for the Infanta, but there was an accident.'

'It was a parrot and he ate it,' the hand said.

'I didn't eat it; it fell into my mouth,' Tom said. He grabbed a mop lying on deck and waved it at the bird.

'What are we going to do?' the hand asked.

'With the captain incapacitated, you will have to assume command,' Tom said, turning to where the mate had been.

'Sorry, what did you say?' While the hand was throwing rubber ducks at the giant bird, the mate had retrieved his mobile phone and was hanging from the side railing with his arm outstretched.

'What are you doing?' Tom said. 'Taking a picture for your mum?'

'This is going directly onto social media,' the mate said. 'It should get loads of hits.'

'You can't do that,' said the hand.

'It isn't against regulations,' the mate replied.

'No, but the reception is rubbish here,' the hand answered.

'Even from the top mast?'

'Perhaps you two humans could discuss broadband later.' Tom jumped as the canvas from the main sail was ripped from the ropes by the roc's beak and came crashing down.

'Watch it,' the mate shouted. 'Repairs don't come cheap.' The sun reflected from the screen of his phone, bouncing a shaft of light into the bird's eyes. It gave a squawk to deafen the nearby humpback whale and swooped down to seize the phone from the mate's hands.

'I think it wants a selfie,' the hand said.

'Quick, while it's distracted,' Tom signalled the mate and the hand to assemble beside him. 'If we all three tug on the wheel, the ship will turn sharply and the roc will fly smack, bang into that rock.'

'That should give it a headache,' the hand observed.

'Ready?'

'Wait,' the mate said.

'What is it?' Tom hissed.

'It's heading for the captain. Unhand him, you beast.'

The bird ignored the mate's frantic hand-flapping and gripped the grandfather clock in its claws. It wrenched the captain free of the ropes then rose into the air with three magnificent flaps and flew off.

'I think it's gone,' Tom said.

'But it has taken the captain,' the mate replied.

'It is only a clock, you know,' the hand said.

'A broken one at that,' Midshipman Tom stared at the mate.

'It could be mended,' the hand suggested.

'Cheaper buying a new one,' said Tom.

'That is not the point.' The mate was almost in tears. 'We are speaking about the ship's captain. What will people say when we arrive in port without him?'

'I wouldn't worry what others say,' Tom said. 'People are always saying catty things about me.'

'That's because you are a cat,' the hand said.

'I shall ignore that remark because we are friends,' Tom huffed. 'I wouldn't take it from anyone else.' He flexed the tips of his fingers to protract sharpened claws.

'Let's not argue,' the mate said. 'We need to rescue the captain.'

'No, we don't,' Tom said.

'You mean a quest?' the hand said. 'We will be legends.'

'I hate quests,' Tom said. 'Especially dangerous ones, where somebody dies.'

'Wouldn't you risk your life for your captain?' the mate asked.

'No. Besides, you said nothing was worth dying for.'

'That was ten minutes ago,' the mate said.

'I'm in, sir.' The hand stood beside the mate.

'See, the boy has more spunk than you, officer,' the mate put a hand on the hand's shoulder.

'I'm a girl, actually,' the hand said.

'Really?' The mate removed his hand.

'Able Sea-girl Becky Buchanan,' she saluted.

'I'm delighted to meet you, Becky. I'm Ship's Mate George Wilton-Watt, or I will be when I officially pass out. My father was Captain Willoughby Watt and my grandfather was Rear Admiral Cloudesly Watt.'

'You've got a Rear Admiral in the family?' Becky was impressed.

'Please, we don't want you passing out too,' Tom said. 'If the introductions are over, can we go to the Infanta's tennis party as planned?'

'Not before we've rescued our captain,' the mate was unflinching.

'But you've only been hired for an hour to guide us into the harbour,' Tom argued.

'An hour will be long enough,' the mate said.

'He's just gutted because he can't be captain,' Becky whispered to the mate.

'I heard that and it's not true,' Tom said.

'We don't have time for squabbling,' said the mate as he marched towards the bow. 'Midshipman, set a course for the beast's lair.'

'Aye, aye sir.'

Tom turned the wheel as Becky sprung into action to haul the main sail into position.

'I'll be below if you need me,' the mate said. He wobbled to the top of the narrow stair leading to the captain's cabin and stopped to pull his stomach and chest in before trying to descend.

'Land ahoy,' the hand called.

'We can't have arrived already,' the mate said.

'You've only got forty five minutes left on your contract,' Tom said. 'We had to fast forward.'

'Are you sure this is the roc's lair? It looks like the Infanta's palace.'

'They are close neighbours,' Tom said.

'They had better be or I'll have you arrested for insub… in … su … disobeying orders,' the mate finished.

'That isn't very nice,' Tom said. 'We are all friends on this ship.'

'It's a friend ship,' the hand agreed.

'I forgave Becky for calling me a cat,' Tom explained.

'What about the captain? Isn't he a friend?' the mate asked.

'Technically, he isn't on the ship,' Becky said.

'And we can be friends without risking our lives,' Tom offered.

'Nobody is going to die,' the mate said.

'We will, at some point,' Becky mused. 'We're not immortal.'

'Of course, we will all die at some point,' the mate agreed.

'Except the captain,' Becky reminded him. 'He's already dead wood.'

'If I die, we are not friends anymore,' Tom said, pointing a claw at the mate.

'You can't say that,' Becky said.

The midshipman curled his lip, then grinned. 'Forty minutes now. We'd better get ashore before you have to report back to HQ.'

'It would be nice to have a long term position,' the mate mused. 'With time to get to know people.'

Tom mumbled something about a double-edged sword, but nobody answered.

'Should I fix the landing ramp?' Becky asked.

'We can leap ashore from here,' Tom said. His back was arched, ready to spring.

'We're not all cats,' the mate complained, before realising his mistake. 'I'm sorry, I didn't say that.'

With a swish of his golden tail that hit the mate on the nose, the midshipman leapt from the vessel onto the pier.

The hand dragged a plank across the deck and manoeuvred it over the side. 'You first, sir.'

'This way,' Tom said as he met the others, now resplendent in white shorts, a white sports top and a sleeveless V-neck sweater. He swished a tennis racket in the air.

'We are going to the roc's lair,' the mate said.

'Won't your white clothes get spoilt?' Becky asked.

'If my clothes get spoilt, what does it matter what colour they are?' Tom said.

While the hand worked out the logic of Tom's remark, they headed up a steep path towards a magnificent, milk-white palace perched precariously on an overhanging cliff. Two mounted sentries guarded the gates.

'Are they what I think they are? Becky asked, looking at Tom.

'You could say they are more centauries than sentries,' Tom agreed.

'We have come to rescue our captain.' The mate puffed out his chest and stepped forward to greet the guards.

'We are expected.' Tom winked.

'Of course. The guests are assembled at the marquee.'

'Guests?' asked the mate.

'For the tennis tournament, sir,' the centaur explained.

'Tom?' said the mate.

'Well, I admit this is the Infanta's palace, but the roc will be here. He wouldn't decline an invitation.'

The gates were opened and the crew were directed into a tiled marble courtyard. A man approached wearing a tweed jacket, plus fours and green woollen socks that looked like they were straight from the loom. He was balancing a shotgun under his right arm.

'Tom, old man,' he greeted the midshipman. 'Are you here for the tennis?'

'Defending my title,' Tom said. 'If I win, it will be seven in a row and I get to keep the trophy.'

'The grandfather clock. Spiffing.'

'There will be no time for games. We are looking for the roc,' the mate said. 'I believe he is a neighbour of yours.'

'A roc?' The gentleman looked perplexed.

'A large bird with fearsome teeth and daggers for claws,' the hand said. 'If it pierces you with its eyes, your bones burn to ashes and, at the touch of a feather, your skin turns to ice.'

The mate and Tom shivered.

'You mean Bertie?' the gentleman said. 'Good man. I play golf with him on Sundays. He is probably terrorising the children or setting fire to barns. You could ask his housekeeper. That's her, beside the cheese.'

'The mouse?' Tom said.

'You think she looks like a mouse?' the man rubbed his chin. 'I have heard people mention the likeness. Don't see it myself.'

'She is about five centimetres tall, has a long tail, mouse fur and whiskers,' Becky said.

'Yes, but calling her a mouse would be like calling Tom here a cat. Ha!' the lord said. 'Must shoot off now.'

'I should speak with the roc's housekeeper. I have a way with ladies.' Tom twirled his whiskers.

'And mice,' Becky added.

The housekeeper was sweeping crumbs of cheese under a chair when Tom leapt up. She jumped back and dropped her broom.

'I hope I didn't frighten you,' Tom purred. 'I was just thinking how delicious you look, with your skirts swaying like that.'

The mouse blushed. 'I bet you say that to all the mice.'

'Not at all.' Tom licked his lips.

'Tom has to go,' Becky interrupted. 'He's due on court to open the tournament. He is the reigning tennis champion.'

The mouse fluttered her eyelashes. Tom was about to lift her in his paws, but Becky poked him in the chest. 'We'll meet you later,' she said. 'After we've seen the roc.'

'The roc? Yes, I would love to stay, but my opponent awaits.' Tom bowed to the housekeeper and darted off.

'What business have you with Sir Bertie?' the housekeeper asked.

'He has something belonging to us: a grandfather clock,'

Becky said.

'The roc is a mythical beast. What need does he have for telling time?' the housekeeper wondered. 'You don't mean the music box he brought home this morning, do you?'

'The music box? Yes, that's it!' Becky smiled.

'Have you come to mend it? The roc is heartbroken he can't get it to sing.'

'Yes,' the mate said, before the hand could answer. He was puffing as he reached them. It had taken him some time to join the hand. The Infanta had waylaid him and insisted on a round of croquet. He had thought it only proper to allow the Infanta to win, but she had insisted on a re-match. 'Do you know where it is?'

'It is in Sir Bertie's private study. I'm only allowed in every second Wednesday to clear the bones and grimy bits of sinew that stick in his teeth.'

'Too much infor …' The mate grabbed the hand's hat and held it over his mouth.

'You will need to get the key from Sir Bertie,' the mouse said.

'Where is he?' Becky asked.

'It's his day to take the pensioners to the bridge,' the housekeeper answered. 'He shouldn't be long. There aren't many pensioners left.'

'I play a little bridge on my days off,' the mate said. 'Perhaps I can make up the numbers.'

Becky gave the mate a nudge, 'I don't think they are playing cards.'

Before them was a river that widened where it met the sea; high above it, in the distance, a shadow hovered several hundred feet above a suspension bridge. Dangling from the beast's legs was a tiny, struggling speck. As they watched, the roc released its grip and the speck dropped like a falling star, knocked against the bridge and rebounded into the water.

'I see,' the mate said. 'What exactly is the point of this

game?'

'It's not a game,' said the housekeeper. 'The skull is cracked open on the bridge and the brains are then easier to pick out.'

'Maybe we should come back on a Wednesday,' Becky said.

'There is another way into the study,' the housekeeper said. 'If you can climb.'

The mate coughed and looked at the hand.

'Tom is the one for serious wall climbing,' Becky said.

'Is there a ladder to the study?' the mate asked.

'Or a fixed fire escape?' the hand added.

'You can climb up Punzel's hair,' the housekeeper offered.

'Punzel?' said the mate and hand together.

'The roc's ward. She's normally very prim and proper but, once she's drunk a few bottles of wine, she'll let her hair down.'

'Do we have any wine, sailor?' the mate asked.

'Only rum, sir.'

'That will do,' the housekeeper said. 'I have to go now. I serve the barley water between sets.'

'Thank you,' the mate said. He turned and handed the hand her hat. 'Get back to the ship and fetch the rum. I'll find this Punzel girl.'

'Aye, aye sir.' Becky replaced her hat and a congealed glob of half-digested bangers and mash slopped down her hair.

'Sorry.' The mate clenched his teeth.

Punzel was brushing tags from her twenty metres of hair when the mate found her.

'Allow me to introduce myself. My name is George ...'

'Whatever. Do you know who is winning the tennis?' Punzel interrupted.

'No, sorry.'

'It's probably the cat. He wins every year. Boring.' Punzel

yawned.

'I guess he's good at tennis.' The mate shrugged.

'I'm rubbish at games, but I do know how to brush hair,' Punzel said.

'You get lots of practise, I'm sure.'

'What is that supposed to mean?' Punzel lowered her brush and took an aggressive step towards the mate.

'Nothing. Why, here's the hand with the rum rations.' The mate backed off.

'About time. I haven't had a drop to drink for hours.'

The hand was staggering under a crate of rum. She dropped it at the mate's feet.

'Careful, you might break something,' the mate and Punzel said, then stared at each other. Punzel helped herself to a bottle and cracked it open with her teeth. The alcohol was downed before the mate could even ask if she wanted a mixer. Punzel burped and reached for another bottle.

'I'm glad you like our rum,' the mate said. 'Perhaps you would be so kind as to do a teeny, weeny, ickle, peedie little favour in return?'

'Like what?' Punzel stopped drinking.

'We need to get into the roc's study to steal …' the hand began.

'Mend …' the mate corrected.

'… to mend the grandfather clock,' the hand finished.

'The music box, she means,' the mate said. 'We want it to be ready when Sir Bertie gets back from the bridge.'

'That's nice of you,' Punzel said.

'We're nice people,' said Becky.

'So you'll help us?' the mate asked.

Punzel choked on the rum. 'I didn't say that. Nobody goes in the roc's study without his permission. Not if they want to come out alive.'

'But if you were to go to your room and lean out the window, your hair might dangle down,' Becky said.

'And you would hardly notice if the lad here climbed up it,' the mate added.

'She's a girl,' Punzel said.

'Of course. I was forgetting.'

'She's got breasts bigger than two stuffed chickens,' Punzel said.

'Has she? I didn't notice,' the mate turned bright crimson.

'You're kind of cute when you do that, Georgie. Tell you what, if I can kiss your cheeks, I'll let you both climb up my hair.'

'Very well,' the mate said, drawing his face closer.

'Not those cheeks.' Punzel smiled to show a mouthful of broken teeth and pus.

The mate's crimson face turned green.

'I'll look away,' Becky said.

Ten minutes later the hand was clambering ahead of the mate up Punzel's hair to the window of the roc's study. There was no glass in the frame so they heaved themselves in.

'I guess the housekeeper hasn't been in for a while,' the hand said, holding the tail of her shirt to her nose.

'What is that?' the mate asked.

'Don't ask. It may once have been attached to some vital organ.'

They squelched across the floor, slipping on layers of jellied offal. Pickled eyes watched them from bottles on the shelves.

'Can you see the captain?' The mate had his eyes closed.

'Over here,' Becky called.

'Is he alive?' the mate said.

The hand put her ear to the clock. 'Barely ticking.'

'Get him to the window,' the mate ordered.

'I can't - he's taller and heavier than me.'

'It's a matter of technique,' the mate said. 'I'll show you.'

'No need. Look who's behind you.'

The mate felt the draught from the roc's wings as it came to rest on the window frame and turned slowly to face the beast.

'Ah good, you've got my phone,' the mate said, spotting the device in the roc's claws. 'Perhaps I could have it back?'

The bird raised its neck and bellowed out a raucous roar.

'Keep it. I need an upgrade anyway.'

The roc stuck out one wing to block the mate's escape.

'We tried to fix your music box, but I'm afraid we'll need to take it to our warehouse for repair,' the hand said.

'We don't have the body parts here,' the mate said.

The bird hopped off its perch, knocking the mate to the floor. His new uniform was splattered with blood and bile. The beast advanced on the hand, making pecking gestures. Becky backed towards the door.

'Steady on,' the mate said, as he climbed to his feet. 'We weren't the ones who broke it.'

'Actually, you were,' Becky said.

'It's probably still under guarantee, so you won't have to pay,' the mate said.

The roc kicked the mate, sending him sprawling back into a pile of rotten fingers. The hand clawed at the door, willing it to open.

'Punzel, can you hear me? We need help. Now!' she called. The roc's beak hurtled towards her. Becky darted out of the way. 'Mrs Mousekeeper? Is anyone there?'

The roc pulled its beak from the door and took aim again. The hand closed her eyes. Before the roc could strike, the door swung open, sending Becky sprawling across the room. She grabbed the roc's tail to prevent herself falling out of the window.

'Am I missing the fun?' Tom said, entering the room.

The roc cocked his head to the side and made a cooing noise. Becky helped the mate to his feet and they scrambled behind Tom.

'Come on, let's go,' the mate urged.

'What about the captain?' Becky said.

'I'm afraid he's a goner.'

Tom moved towards the captain, taking care not to get any mess on his tennis whites. The roc had its eyes fixed on the object Tom was carrying.

'This old music box is broken,' Tom said. 'We can dispose of it free of charge and in exchange we can replace it with a brand new, mega shiny, working model.' He signalled to the hand to move the captain, then set the tennis trophy in its place. 'Listen to this.' Tom twirled the hands of the clock he had just won. The chime rang out and the roc danced a jig.

'Excellent moves, Sir Bertie,' Tom said, backing out the door.

The mate was already at the stairs, with the hand struggling to pull the captain after her.

'Allow me,' said Tom.

'What, you are actually going to do some manual work?' Becky said.

'Not at all.' Tom raised his claws to his mouth and gave a whistle. Before the last note squeezed out, three mice were scrambling round the hand's legs. More joined them until the corridor was a blanket of brown fur. Between them they lifted the captain and marched towards the stairs.

'I have a way with mice,' Tom said.

'Let me guess,' said the hand, scratching her head in an exaggerated manner, 'you threatened to eat them?'

'I asked for a little favour.'

'You call entering the roc's house and removing his grandfather clock a little favour?' the mate said.

'Well, they are only little chaps,' Tom said.

Behind them, they could hear the clang of the new grandfather clock chiming, followed by a thud as the roc practised his pas de chat. The mate sucked through his teeth. 'Just as well you won, Tom.'

'It was never in doubt,' Tom retorted. 'Pity I'll have to win the tournament another seven times before I can keep my prize.'

'You saved the captain, that's what matters,' the mate said.

Tom was about to reply, but they had reached the ship and the mice were waiting for instructions on where to deposit the captain. Tom sprang on board to direct them and they managed to shuffle the clock against the main mast.

'Excellent job, chaps,' said Tom, and dismissed them.

The hand had to quickly step aside to avoid being knocked into the water by a wave of fleeing rodents. She joined Tom on the deck, but the mate remained dawdling on the pier.

'Aren't you coming, sir?' Tom called.

'My work is finished,' the mate said.

'There are still four minutes left,' the hand said.

'Or longer if you go by the captain's time-keeping,' Tom added.

'Well, I suppose I should sign off properly,' the mate said, straightening his uniform before stepping aboard. The hand secured the captain to the mast and they all saluted.

'Good work, men,' the mate proclaimed. 'I'm proud to have served with you.'

'The captain is in position, but he is still broken,' Tom said. 'We need a new commander.'

'Surely you will stand in?' The mate screwed his hands in his pockets.

'The crew would prefer you,' replied Tom.

'I don't mind who is captain,' Becky said before Tom stamped on her toes.

'You did say you would like a permanent position,' Tom said.

'Why yes. I would be honoured, if nobody minds,' the mate responded.

The captain, of course, said nothing, and Becky was too busy hopping around the deck to object.

'Welcome aboard, captain,' Tom saluted. 'The ship is ready for her next adventure.'

'Very good. Pull her hard to starboard.'

'Hard to starboard it is, sir.'

DARK FANTASY

THE SPECTRE OF SAN ESTRADUS

By James Agombar

I. DARK CLOUDS

April 16th 1992: Hayman burned the tyres of the 1989 Plymouth Gran Fury into town, but was still late for the meeting. The radio broadcast had declared that 'a reign of suspicion and paranoia' had recently been cast over the tired desert town of San Estradus, just south of West Virginia. A string of reports had called on the Interstate Investigation Department (IID) to look into the disappearance of a thirteen-year old boy.

Hayman had little time for people as a pessimist, but intended to crack every case wide open nonetheless. He had been told that he was being partnered with Detective Michelle Easton for this one, who was due to arrive later from another assignment.

San Estradus was a dusty, square town, with two roads in and out, from the north and south. The highway led straight along for miles before the town appeared as a clustered speck in the distance. The road kill depleted significantly as he approached its entrance. It was decorated with a solitary pathetic welcoming sign: "San Estradus – Welcome".

The wind was whistling in varying pitches, brief and unsettled. Dust devils whirled at the barren edges of the town. The clouds overhead were dark and backlit by flashes of lightning, like a hurricane was pending. He passed long empty spaces entering into town, as if he'd just missed an exodus.

Signs of life flicked by as Alex cranked down the window. Rundown motels, trailer homes, a half empty gas station with pumps from the fifties and a closed diner. Several large dogs barked from behind a chain-link fence as he turned right at the south-east corner of the town. He travelled a little further west, to where the meeting point was and, in a few minutes he was at the south-west junction, where an old cinema was crumbling. Flecks of paint peeled from beneath the tattered neon sign at the top of its entrance. Large, red letters spelt out the word "Cineplex", with the "L" missing. It looked like it hadn't been lit for some time.

He pulled up outside, flicked the engine off and stepped out of the car. It didn't seem necessary to find an official parking space.

A tumbleweed brushed past his foot and on down the road. He glanced in the direction it had come from and noticed the mountains in the distance, past the trees. A circle of dark cloud spun atop the mountain and storm flies were gathered in droves. It seemed far enough away to cause the town no harm but near enough to display one hell of a show if it was active.

He reached inside his jacket pocket and pulled a cigarette from its case. Holding one in his mouth, he reached into the car through the open window and brought out the lighter from the glove box. The wind started to kick up and it failed to light, so he returned the cigarette to its box and stepped toward the cinema.

Through the creaky double doors, the reception resembled a Wild West style cinema from the 1890's. A small sign was perched next to the bar, held in place by a wispy spine of metal, with an arrow on it directing to the town council meeting. He followed the sign and passed through another set of doors into the auditorium. The musty air clogged his lungs; it was damp and coarse, as if the place had a few leaks. It was dark inside and a silent movie was flicking by on the big screen. Several figures were silhouetted against it. Luckily, the meeting was just about to begin, but he could sense that something wasn't right. He stood quietly just inside the door to listen.

The screen flashed a cycle of images with characters interacting, babies crying, missiles launching from silos, tanks rolling over trenches, an eerie old church with a rickety gate swinging in the wind, and a woman screaming. The woman had a face that was normal one moment and then evil the next, as if one moment she was the victim and the next the aggressor. Hayman screwed his face up, not understanding any of it.

Gradually, his eyes adapted to the darkness and began to make out the faces of the people gathered there. He listened in on the speaker's voice more closely.

'Good Afternoon. My name is Frank Dowman, Chief of San Estradus law enforcement. It is clear this town needs help and its citizens would greatly appreciate it from you all. You are probably all wondering what style of meeting this is but I'm afraid I hold no answers. I ask you group of bounty hunters, investigators, do-gooders and brave citizens to conduct your own methods of engagement and collaborate with each other on this. To aid you in this matter may I present to you, Professor Joshua Barkley, who has some background information on current events.'

The chief had a voice that bore experience, and at the same time, a hint of desperation. The man he had introduced walked on stage with no applause. The professor's voice was different, informative and slow; a droll, Brooklyn accent that was odd for these parts. He was a young guy with shoulder length blonde hair; not a look you would associate with a scientist.

'Welcome, ladies and gentlemen. A great force seems to have overcome this town and, being a scientist, I suspect that this may be something of a setup, or manmade corruption. However, despite my beliefs, I respect that some people have faith in the supernatural or paranormal.' He held up a report in his right hand, the writing on it indecipherable at that distance. 'This is a report on the recent event, from an eyewitness who has been crosschecked by a historian in this room. It tells of a venture into the woods to the south four days ago. The witness took his son with him, a young boy by the name of Trent Sedriss. They attempted a return from a hunting trip to their vehicle when the rain started to come. Soon they realised they were lost and it became too dark to navigate. With only small torches to hand, they persisted and then heard what they thought were gunshots from a certain area. Hoping that another hunter was nearby, they followed the sounds, which became louder and more terrifying than mere gunshots. The sounds were coming from the mountain, and deepened as they got closer.'

'Surely it was the sound of the mountain spitting!' interrupted one voice.

'It has been known to be active at certain times of the year!' shouted another.

'As you say, that is possible, but the sounds he described he assures were not the sound a mountain would make; they were much sharper explosions, like glass breaking or kids playing with firecrackers. They came to an opening through the trees, and realised the mountain was very close; apparently at this time the boy claimed he could hear manic laughter echoing from the crater. As they peered through the trees, they searched for a figure. Trent's father claims he saw and heard nothing like laughter. The crater hissed and spat small rocks, but not in time with the firecracker-like sound. The boy became terrified and assured his father that he could see a figure, and the laughter was that of a woman.' The scientist started to read from the report directly now. 'A woman who laughed in a foreboding manner and was only visible in silhouette form, dancing at the top of the crater, wearing what seemed to be rags. Her body grew larger and her voice also became magnified.'

'How old is the boy?' a large man with folded arms questioned.

'Thirteen,' replied Joshua.

'That report was too wordy for a thirteen-year old. Who wrote this?' asked another man to his left.

He was tall and thin and wearing a gunbelt. Hayman definitely saw his point.

'By all means, please let me finish and I will take questions afterwards,' the scientist continued. 'The father has reiterated his interactions with his son for this report because, at this point he claims that the boy became too frightened to investigate any further, or even stand still. He panicked and ran into the woods screaming. Trent's father pursued the boy for what he believes to be approximately three hours, well into the early hours of Sunday morning. At approximately six a.m. of that morning, the father appeared at the police station to report his son missing, exhausted and terrified. The only word he could repeat in certainty for some time was, "Makutu",' he finished.

Hayman folded his arms in contemplation. He thought that the whole story seemed to be caked in mystic bullshit that only gathered any credence in isolated towns like this. He was still unsure what he, or the other people in the room, were meant to investigate exactly. He just hoped at this point that this wasn't going to turn into a mountain hike or a hunt for the kid in dumpsters and basements.

'So where do you suggest as a good point of interest?' asked someone in a high and quivering voice near the back of the cinema.

Hayman's gaze shifted from the voice back to the scientist again.

'The people of San Estradus will be willing to co-operate,

but I suggest a joint endeavour to the crater, on account of the following information delivered to us by our local historian, Miss Alexandra Lappentti.' He gestured one arm in the direction of a figure that was mostly hidden within the dark void of the auditorium. 'She warned us of an old myth from Polynesia where a form of discipline was used to scaremonger the lower classes. This force is known as "makutu", and is of Maori descent. The nearest translation known to us is the word "witchcraft". There have been many references to makutu over the centuries but the most significant and most recent was in 1987 on the atoll of Faaite, in the South Pacific. The locals were visited by three women claiming to be missionaries for the Catholic Church, looking to provide education. After weeks of daily services, the leader of the three women preached that God had left their island and that demons were in their midst. The local islanders went on a hunt, terrified that their loved ones were about to be possessed by supernatural forces. The torture and killing of six that followed led to twenty-three people being sentenced, all of whom believed that they were acting in the name of God to rid their land of those possessed by demons.'

Hayman's brow creased and he wondered how all this was linked. 'Some sort of fucking witch hunt now?' he muttered under his breath.

Another gentleman, hidden in the shadowy seating area, raised his hand. 'Excuse me, not ruling out the possibility of Witchcraft, would you suggest we call in an expert on this type of thing? And even if that is the case, is the point of this investigation to resolve supernatural activity, or to find the missing child?'

The scientist blinked rapidly. 'I'm afraid I will have to pass you over to Miss Lappentti now. She is a supernatural specialist and more of an expert on this type of thing. However, the main objective is to recover the minor alive, with any possible circumstances remaining second in line. Thank you,' he said, and stepped back into the group of people near the front.

Lappentti stepped up to replace Joshua. She had long, frizzy hair and her body language was much more animated than Joshua's.

'Good Afternoon. Days after the sentencings, a fourteen-year old boy on the island of Faaite reported that his aunt had been possessed through the use of makutu. The boy claimed she had been neglecting her regular routine and taken to dancing up the mountain located at the centre of the atoll. We don't know for certain that she survived but she was the first of four to be subjected to an island-wide exorcism. These exorcisms were conducted by Tohungas, high priests who specialise in ejecting demons. The entire region gathered in prayer around each subject for several nights to perform these,' she said.

This was certainly something that was outside Hayman's line of duty, although recently there had been a blurring of the lines when it came to what his duties were. One thing was certain though, he had had enough of this chicken shit story already and was dying for a cigarette, so he decided to discreetly light up.

Another male voice piped up, offering a "hands-on" approach. 'So that's the way forward now! We find the boy, and he might lead us to the witch; then we perform an exorcism with your guidance,' he said, making it sound so simple.

'I'm sorry but I'm not qualified to do exorcisms and it's not likely to be that straightforward either,' she replied. 'Dr Barkley believes this event to be a standard fear-and-strike kidnapping which I hope each and every one of you will believe for now. My evidence suggests something more tricky but equally plausible.'

Hayman had started shifting from one leg to the other,

blowing smoke in front of the big screen that was still flashing with the strange images.

'Legends tell that the first to fall prey to makutu is always a woman. Then a male, or perhaps even a young boy, bears witness to these things that others may find hard to see themselves. If I am correct then it is likely the missing boy ran away because the demon he witnessed was in possession of a woman,' Lappentti added.

The same voice replied, 'So, you're saying there's a female witch at large?'

'So it seems,' the historian replied forlornly.

Quite a portion of the crowd started to grow restless with this whole explanation. It was certainly not what they had prepared for. Hayman just shook his head.

'It is now Thursday 21st April and the child hasn't been found. Please take these cards,' Lappentti said, handing them out. 'If anybody finds any new information, please stay in touch with the police department here. It has been expanded temporarily to conduct this search.'

Chief Dowman brought the meeting to a close. 'Best of luck ladies and gentlemen. We must use everything at our disposal to find these children. Communication is key!'

Hayman stubbed out the cigarette in a nearby ashtray bin as the film finished and the lights came on. He turned to walk to the exit rather than sticking around to speak with what he had decided was a bunch of hicks with pitchforks. He took a contact card from a guy who was handing them out at the entrance and walked back to his car.

Sliding behind the driver's seat of the Gran Fury, he lit another cigarette and glanced at the storm gathered above the intimidating mountain. 'A fucking witch!' he said, shaking his head. He started the car and drove off to find the motel the IID had booked for him.

II. TWO COINS

The motel was basic. Wooden decking trailed around a courtyard which led to each of the seven rooms. Hayman pulled up around 6pm. The owner was sitting behind the reception desk staring up at a portable TV. He was a fat, greasy haired man with thick lenses and aftershave not too dissimilar to off-milk. Hayman took the keys as the guy started asking questions.

'So, you from the IID, yeah? Thought there were two o' you coming into town?'

'There are. The other will be here shortly; she will need a separate room.'

'Ah, o' course, friend,' he replied, with an inane smile. He leaned in closer over the counter, 'but uh, if you like I could … ya know, say we're all booked out, then she'd have to bunk up with you. You dig what I'm sayin'?'

Hayman just stared at him and raised an eyebrow behind his brown aviators. He wondered why the IID had booked him such sleazy accommodation, but then he remembered how low down on the list this case was. Also, from driving through the town, he suspected that this may be one of the few functioning motels. 'Thanks, but I like my own space,' he replied.

'Sure thing, fella. ID please.'

Hayman flipped his badge open and the owner took down the numbers. 'Can you let the other agent know which room I'm in when she gets here, please?'

'Oh, not sure about that, fella. Data Protection and all that,' he replied with another crooked smile, 'Just kiddin' ya there, heh heh.'

Hayman took the keys and followed the creaky decking to room seven.

An hour later, Hayman was sitting in a chair outside the

door to his room with a beer, reading over the case files. The local authority had also posted him some information about the situation of the victim's family. Nothing seemed out of place in the time leading up to the disappearance. The circumstances surrounding Trent Sedriss had sparked a local search party to head into the woods near the mountain each morning, despite the warnings to avoid the mountain itself.

His thoughts were broken as a vehicle pulled up outside the reception; a faded crimson Buick. A woman in a suit stepped out of the passenger seat, her blonde hair tied back tightly and a skirt that showed her slender figure off. As she waved the driver off, she adjusted her rectangular glasses and headed in to reception. Her name was Michelle Easton. Hayman remembered her from around a year ago when he had last been assigned to work with her, on a case linked to a cargo ship smuggling diamonds into West Virginia. He didn't move from the chair to greet her when recalling her attitude: stuck up and formal. Hayman had got the impression she thought a lot of herself, despite her being new to the job back then. Distance from her would be a welcome factor for this case.

After checking in, she came over to Hayman to reintroduce herself. Her confidence was more solid than her step in high heels as she got one caught in a gap in the decking.

'Good evening, Mr. Hayman,' she said.

'Once again, a pleasure, Miss Easton. Call me Alex, it's fine.'

'Thanks, Alex,' she replied, extending her hand to shake. 'Call me Michelle, or otherwise, Ms. Easton,' she requested.

'Yes ma'am,' Hayman sighed.

'Have you received the details of the case?'

Hayman took a deep breath, stood up and waved the case notes in front of her. 'You'd better come inside and check this out.'

Two days of investigation followed. In that time, the local search party found the boy dead in the woods, with no signs of struggle or poisoning. He was fully clothed, but with a single slice to the left wrist and two unidentified silver coins placed on his eyes. The coins were quarters, but modified and impressed on the eagle side by what appeared to be a circular disk. It left the face blank with a central, raised notch. Some suspicion was still fixed on the father but many had ideas of something more sinister. A local shaman had convinced the police of foul play involving makutu, which was coincidently what the father had apparently unknowingly scrawled across his written statement whilst still in shock.

Given the circumstances, the morgue had the body placed on ice rather than buried. Chief Dowman gave consent for a spiritual investigation in order to retrace events through a local shaman, seeing as there was little other evidence to go on. The shaman had agreed to make the ritual of contact public so that witnesses could give statements if necessary. The meeting point was just outside town, behind the old cinema. Hayman and Easton knew that they had to attend, regardless of the outcome.

Behind the cinema, they followed the dirt track and parked in the brush. A pointed rock marked a sacred location that the shaman had selected. A fire had been lit before it.

Upon reaching the area, Hayman lit a cigarette and stood waiting. A small crowd of strangers, including two policemen, stood around in an arc watching warily.

The shaman carried the body through the crowd and set it down in front of the smouldering fire. The two coins had been placed back on the eyes of the corpse.

Hayman noticed an old woman, with thin grey hair,

amongst the crowd as it parted. When she stepped back, she dropped some change on the ground. A young man retrieved it for her.

The shaman was Mexican; around six-foot-six with veins running down his arms like rivers, parting his dark, leathery skin. Wrapped in a poncho and walking on tattered sandals, he waved a stick around maniacally and chanted up into the night sky. He sprinkled dust over the body in front of him. The fire behind the corpse grew and embers floated up, concealing the stars. "Spirit, fury, fire," he chanted repeatedly. He lowered the stick, then placed his hands, one over the other, on the body and applied pressure. His humming was muffled slightly by the dark hair that hung past his shoulders.

Hayman tapped his foot impatiently and burned through the cigarette between his lips. 'Fucking CPR now?' he muttered under his breath.

Easton was stood with her arms wrapped around her waist, as if in pain. 'Have some respect!' she snapped, tapping his arm.

Hayman just looked at her. He thought that respect would have been better paid by not inviting a shaman to play séance with the body.

Easton noted the absence of Trent's father, but could understand why. She rubbed her glasses for a clearer view.

The crowd grew restless as the shaman started to babble incoherently in Mexican. Some people started to back away slowly, while others looked on in amazement.

The shaman sat back, away from the body as the fire began to burn blue. The wind kicked up and he started to convulse. Down on all fours, he bowed his head before lifting it again with frosted eyes and stained, snapping teeth. His breathing was becoming laboured. A few amongst the crowd grew concerned and stepped forward to help, but they were greeted with growls and spittle.

'This doesn't look right,' said Easton, shaking her head.

'It's just an act. You're not really buying this Mickey Mouse bullshit are you?' replied Hayman.

Guttural noises that sounded like cracking glass crept from the shaman's open mouth. Suddenly he stood and stared straight at Hayman, who in return tried to stare him down.

'I knew this was a bad idea,' Easton sputtered, backing away.

The shaman spat through his teeth in a language that was neither Mexican, nor English. Then, without warning, he thrust forward from the chest, as if by an explosion, and hurtled towards Hayman.

The cigarette dropped from Hayman's lips as he instinctively unholstered and raised his gun. 'Stand down!' he warned.

The shaman continued to charge with eager hands flung out, reaching for Hayman's neck.

The gunshot echoed for miles.

Hayman suffered a black eye after being tackled. Some of the nearest onlookers pulled the shaman away and he fell unconscious shortly afterward. Doctors noted that, strangely, the shaman hadn't complained of any pain from the wound after being admitted to San Estradus Hospital for a bullet to the left thigh. He suffered no broken bones and was released within the week. While in custody, he claimed that the coins had "blocked his vision", resulting in his possession by a demon of ancient Polynesian descent. He also claimed to have no recollection of the event after he had started chanting. Chief Cohen requested that his two agents return to West Virginia within the next three days, as speculation about the coins being cursed left the case in a farcical position. The only positive part of the situation was that Trent's father was given some closure with a decent burial for his son.

Hayman was sporting a few bruises on his torso that reminded him to move slowly as he sat up, but he ignored the bodily warnings and ended up knocking an empty bottle of Jim Beam off the bed. His brow creased as he caught sight of himself in the mirror on top of the dresser.

Someone knocked on motel room door. He opened it to find Easton with a scowl on her face, dressed for business

'We need to get out of here. I can't think properly in this place anymore,' she said, brushing past him and plucking the car keys from the dresser.

'I couldn't agree more.'

'Two more days and they won't fund us being out here anymore.'

'Right. So why do you look so pissed off about it? Just relax.'

She spun on her heels to face him and threw his shirt at him, urging him to get dressed.

'Because I have new evidence … and I can't talk Cohen around into pursuing it. He's shelving the case.'

Hayman sneered and reached for the door key.

'I don't like this case much, but I like Cohen even less.'

Easton checked her watch. 'Shit. Come on, you need to see this. Breakfast is on me,' she said.

Easton bought them each a coffee at a local diner, and picked a window seat for them with a clear view. 'See that guy?' she asked, pointing out the window.

'Yeah.'

'I woke early this morning and took a walk. I ended up across the street where that man is,' she said, pointing out a beggar who was sitting cross-legged outside a minimart, holding a cup. His clothes were ripped and he had long grey hair down to his waist. A pair of dark, round glasses perched on his nose; one of the lenses was cracked. A dog was slumped over his left knee.

'Yeah, so what?'

'So, as I was grabbing a drink from the vendor next to him, he started complaining about how Vietnam veterans shouldn't be disrespected with phoney money. When I asked what he meant, he showed me his coffee cup, which was full of change, and he gave me some of these. He said I could keep them as evidence because no businesses or automated machines would accept it.'

Michelle dropped a small bag of change on the table, filled with quarters with the same imprints as those that had been placed on the eyes of the deceased boy.

'Did you ask him who gave them to him?'

'He's blind.'

'Right.'

'But he said he'd do me a favour; he's doing it right now. He said that most coins are dropped in his cup mid-morning. I said I'd keep watch at that time. He'll feel the coins over and, if any of them have the same marks, he'll give me the thumbs up.'

Alex raised his eyebrows and lit a cigarette. It seemed all they had to do was wait it out.

Barely twenty minutes had passed and already five people had dropped coins into his Styrofoam cup. They watched eagerly as he felt each of the coins in turn, but no thumbs up. Another cigarette had burned down to the stub in Hayman's mouth when a young girl skipped by in a dress and dropped some coins into his cup. The beggar gave the signal.

'What, this doesn't make any sense; she's what … eight years old?' Hayman ranted.

Easton wasn't listening and hurried across the road to check with the beggar. She handed him a twenty-dollar note and gave Hayman a thumbs up.

Hayman ditched the coffee and rushed to fetch the car, so they could follow the girl from a distance.

III. INNOCENCE

The agents followed the girl into Yellow Bird Trailer Park. A rusty, gilded sign formed an archway above the entrance, like an evil rainbow. The wheel felt heavier as he drove along the uneven dirt tracks. A burnt out pickup truck sat to the left, sheltering a handful of chickens.

Hayman glanced quizzically at Michelle and she returned a despairing look.

'There she is, just on the right, around this corner,' said Michelle, pointing.

He turned the corner and pulled up outside the trailer home she had entered into - number 84.

Michelle noticed a man sitting on a deckchair outside the trailer opposite, watching them. He was skinny, around fifty, and wore an old army cap. A thin, lit cigarette hung from his lips.

Number 84 was an early eighties design with grass growing in tall patches around the drawbar. A group of oil drums stood outside the flimsy panelling around the door and wind chimes littered the air with tinkling noises as they approached. Alex toed at one of the diminishing tires propping up the base of the trailer home on one edge, then knocked on the door and put on his brown aviators to hide the black eye.

The door creaked open a few inches, revealing the little girl. She had short, brown plaited hair and a face of innocence.

'Hey there. Is your mom home?' asked Easton.

'My mom's dead. Who are you?' she replied, as she eyed them both.

'We're detectives from the Interstate Investigation

Department of West Virginia, honey. Like police officers.' Easton showed her I.D card.

'You look like a detective, but he doesn't,' replied the girl, pointing to Hayman's civilian clothing.

Easton just looked at him and frowned, not sure what to say about his rugged attire.

'So who do you live with, sweetie?'

'My grandma,' she yawned, 'but she's not home now.'

'Do you mind if we come in and take a look around?'

'Grandma says I shouldn't let strangers in the house.'

'It's very important though, sweetie. I'm sure she wouldn't mind.'

'Hmm … all right, but you can't touch anything, ok. If Grandma finds out I let you in she'll kill me when she gets back.'

'It's ok sweetie, we won't touch a thing, will we, Detective Hayman?' Easton said, looking pointedly at Alex, then back at the girl. 'What's your name?'

'Joanna. What do you want with Grandma?'

'Can you tell us where she is, Joanna? It's very important, honey,' Easton replied.

'She went shopping; she won't be back for a while. She says I really shouldn't let strangers inside, you know,' Joanna said, shaking her head.

Inside they were greeted with an armchair covered in old blankets and two bookshelves to the left. Both had the vinegary scent that old library books gain with age. In the centre of the home was a kitchen top that had been converted into a study desk. It was covered with half melted candles and books.

Hayman took his aviators off and gazed up, noticing a set of tribal masks hanging from the wall. They appeared to have been carved from wood. The thick, metal stove burner they were hanging above looked ancient to him.

'Did your grandma carve those?' he asked.

'No. Grandpa brought them to her from the other side of the world. They're very old … I think.'

'Where's Grandpa right now?' asked Easton.

'He died a long time ago. He's in this old photo,' replied Joanna, pointing to a framed photograph sitting on top of an old record deck that was covered in dust.

Easton picked it up to inspect. It showed a young man posing next to a light biplane. 'Looks like this was taken in the thirties maybe,' she figured. 'He must have flown a long way to find these masks, huh?'

Joanna just shrugged.

Easton managed to distract Joanna by asking more questions and getting her to show her the bedroom through the back. As soon as they were gone, Alex sifted lightly through some of the belongings strewn about the place. He wasn't sure where to start. His eyes were drawn to several quarters, scattered underneath a dream catcher, with the same design as the ones that had been dropped into the homeless guy's cup. Amongst them were also small stone discs with holes in them. Picking up a coin and one of the discs, he pressed them together and it became clear that the stones had been imprinted onto the coins somehow. The central hole formed the raised centre of the coins, smothering out the eagle emblem. Underneath the coins was a large, untitled book. He brushed the coins and discs off its cover and flicked through it. The book was written in a language he didn't recognise; there were also several sketches of idols, trees and masks set out in black ink that bled across the pages as he turned them. Amongst the pages was a small device, cylindrical and made out of treated wood. He raised it closer to inspect and saw that it was a vial. He shook it and something inside it shifted. Suddenly, he heard a click as the door behind him opened.

'Hey, what are you doing?' the girl exclaimed.

He turned and saw that she was pointing a pistol at him and trembling. Hayman slowly raised his arms. 'Easy, little girl. No harm done.'

'You promised you wouldn't touch anything!'

Easton rushed back through from the bedroom and looked understandably shocked when she saw the gun. She looked quizzically at Hayman. 'What did he do, sweetie?'

'He broke his promise. You can't mess around with Grandma's hobby stuff. If she finds out, she's going to be real mad. You both need to get out now.'

Hayman left without question as Joanna opened the door for him.

Easton followed whilst trying to settle the girl. 'I'm sorry, Joanna. I'll make sure he doesn't come back. If you could tell Grandma that I'll be back to see her this time tomorrow, I'd appreciate it,' she said, leaving a contact card on the table.

The girl didn't reply and locked the door behind them.

The midday heat forced him to crank the windows down as they stepped back into the car.

'Where'd she get the gun from?' Hayman asked.

'Didn't see. She must have pulled it from a drawer when I wasn't looking.'

Both agents exhaled, feeling cheated.

'You in for this?' Hayman asked.

'Uh-uh. You?'

'No way. Full of freaky shit. These coins match the originals,' he said, pulling one of them from his pocket. Placing his glasses back on, he rolled his gaze to the left. The thin neighbour, resplendent in his tired shirt and cap, was still sprawled in his deckchair. 'Maybe we should talk to Mopey Joe over there and see if he knows anything.'

'Leave it to me,' Michelle insisted, stepping out of the car to question him.

Hayman sat for a moment and pondered the coins,

turning one over in his hand before taking the vial from the front pocket of his jeans. The markings on it seemed random and uneven, as if carved with a hunting knife, but the cylinder was well made. A fibrous string was wrapped around the top of it, attached to a flimsy cork. He spent a few moments studying it before unwinding the string and clumsily pulling the cork open while it was horizontal. Dark red liquid spilt from the lid over his jeans. 'Shit, what the hell?' he exclaimed.

Suddenly a long scream erupted from the trailer home. It started like a child's, and then distorted into the sound of cracking glass.

He leapt out of the car, gun raised, and ran to the trailer. The vial dropped to the ground.

Easton had also heard the screams, and sprinted over, her own gun raised.

Hayman reached the door first and tried the handle. Locked. He aimed and fired at the mechanism. Easton pulled it open for him. A figure slumped across the floor brought them to a halt. Hayman was startled to see that it was the old lady he had seen before, back at the shaman's public ritual. 'Shit,' he said, kneeling beside her and checking her pulse. She was dead.

'Who is she?' asked Easton.

'The woman from the crowd. Is the girl still here?'

Easton checked the back bedroom.

'Nothing, but the neighbour told me he's never known of a little girl living here.'

Alex frowned and stared down at the stain from the dark liquid he had spilt on his jeans.

Three days later, the incidents of San Estradus were written up and reported by all involved. Hayman and Easton were seated in the Chief of Police's office. Present were Chief Dowman, the shaman who had performed the exorcism,

Professor Joshua Barkley and Alexandra Lappentti. Chief Cohen had also dialled in and was tuned in over the loudspeaker of the phone on Dowman's desk. A tape was rolling inside a recorder to document the still confidential reports. Hayman shifted uncomfortably in his chair, which he thought was much too hard, and made to light up a cigarette.

'I'd prefer it if you didn't smoke in here, Detective,' said Dowman.

Hayman eyed him, lighter held close to the tip of the cigarette, and then lowered it. 'Of course … my bad.'

'Professor Barkley, can I have your official report on the situation please,' Dowman requested.

Barkley read from a clipboard in his droll tone. 'Forensics confirmed that the body found in trailer home eighty-four was the body of Rachel Denver, widow of Frank Denver. Their daughter is confirmed as Mary Denver, who passed away in 1975, at the age of thirty-six, from tuberculosis. There is no bloodline for a granddaughter or any relative by the name of Joanna recorded. The coins, found to have fingerprints matching Mrs Denver's, were legal tender U.S quarters, modified and imprinted with an ancient Polynesian currency. The currency, known as Rai stones, were imprinted onto the quarters defacing the eagle emblem side and were probably brought back by Frank Denver during his expeditions to that region. The blood in the vial that Agent Hayman found was confirmed to be that of Trent Sedriss, the missing boy.'

'Thank you, Professor,' Dowman said. 'Miss Lappentti?'

'Good Afternoon. My research confirms supernatural activity, which does not conflict with Professor Barkley's findings. The textbooks in Denver's trailer home seem to have been written by an unknown researcher, making reference to Polynesian stories and theories on witchcraft. The vial we mentioned before is a well-documented vessel for supernatural essence. It is of a kind that has been known to be used to seal spells of significant evil throughout four continents. The girl you saw was possibly an incarnation of Rachel Denver. The discs that were used to imprint on the quarters originate from Micronesia, specifically a northern group of Polynesian culture. They were broken and buried due to being contaminated by makutu, according to elder tribesmen. Some of the island nations suffered economic crises and recession during these times. How Mr Denver acquired them is unknown. Fortunately, the coins don't seem to be in circulation in San Estradus.' Miss Lappenti glanced down at the report in her hand and continued. 'Some theories say that leaving coins on the eyes of the dead is payment for the gods to allow a body to pass through purgatory and on to a final resting place. However, this is more common in European mythology, rather than Polynesian, so the real motive for this remains uncertain. Rachel Denver was likely using a spell to imitate the child form of Joanna, which was broken when Agent Hayman spilled the vial's contents. The speed of the break proved fatal to the woman, it seems.'

'Thank you, Miss Lappentti. Agent Hayman; Detective Easton - do you have anything to add from your official reports?'

Both replied that they didn't. Easton was eager to leave whilst Hayman looked unimpressed and observed that the whole case seemed to be tilted against them. He hadn't bought the witchcraft explanations from day one, but was forced to admit that there was little evidence to support anything else.

The shaman sat attentively, hands clasped together, shrapnel in leg, nodding with each report.

Cohen closed the case under the weak heading of foul play with the blame placed squarely on Rachel Denver. He also told his agents to return home, as the state wasn't willing to spend any more time on this. He was satisfied that no threat remained.

The following morning, the agents checked out of the motel. The shaman stood waiting for them as Alex loaded their bags and closed the trunk. They shook hands and the shaman spoke of his deep regret for his attack on Hayman.

'It couldn't be helped. I don't really go in for all this shit, but I'm certain you weren't in your right mind when you attacked me. I'm sorry about your leg. Seems to be healing fast though,' said Hayman, looking down at the hole in the shaman's dusty jeans.

'I have ways of healing; do not worry about me. I wish you both the very best for your return and bless you for helping our town in these strange times,' replied the shaman.

The agents left, thinking it was an easy retreat for the department, and were certain that the case remained unsolved.

Easton took the wheel, back to West Virginia while the town disappeared in the rearview.

Hayman cranked down the passenger window, lit a cigarette, and watched the cacti and weeds gradually recede, as they got closer to civilisation. He clicked the radio on; a news broadcaster was announcing that the "reign of suspicion and paranoia" had been lifted from San Estradus. He shook his head.

The shaman watched as they drove away, then took a long suck of air, and smiled. Turning and limping west towards the other side of town, he passed a minimart with a beggar sitting cross-legged outside it. The man, who was perhaps sixty, was wearing a pair of dark glasses with one cracked lens.

'Spare some change for a Vietnam vet?' the beggar called out. 'The country didn't give me much back, so I ask of the

people.'

The shaman pulled out a handful of coins and dropped them into his hand.

'God bless you. You're the kind of person I fought for,' the beggar said. He went quiet as he felt an eerily familiar imprint on the side of one of the coins.

The shaman limped away into the distance towards the mountain, which was still covered by dark clouds.

ORIN SLEW

BY JOSEPH DEGAND

Janie never swore but the word "shit" woke Ben from the slumber he'd slipped into on the two-hour drive home from Manchester.

'What's the matter,' he groaned, rubbing his eyes.

'The GPS and my phone lost signal ages ago and there were road works on the dual carriageway,' she explained. 'So I had to turn off and follow diversion signs.'

'Okay, okay – it's not a big deal. Just relax.'

'Relax? It's two o'clock in the morning and I have no idea where we are, Ben…'

He could tell she was getting stressed and worried. The tears were starting to well up in her eyes. Ben looked down at his phone, but it didn't have signal either.

He reached over and gently rubbed her leg, saying, 'It's okay, babe. Calm down and follow signs pointing us towards Lincoln or anywhere else near home. Do you know where we are now?'

'I really don't. I think I saw a sign that said Tuxton a little while ago, but I'm not sure.'

There was really no telling where they were. Outside was just a vast expanse of blackness broken up by the occasional street light. Lincolnshire was known for its farmlands, so the emptiness surrounding them was nothing unexpected.

'Hmm, never heard of it. Look, though. We're coming up to a sign up there.'

Janie eased to a standstill at the intersection. The closest street light was fifty or sixty yards back, so the sign ahead was lit only by their headlights.

What really stood out about it was the boldly scripted graffiti at the top that read – ORIN SLEW – in harsh, red letters.

'No Lincoln on there, but Newark's to the right. Close enough, no?' said Ben.

'I guess,' answered Janie as she started to steer the car right.

'This isn't ideal, is it? Do you want me to drive?'

'No, that's okay. I'll be alright. I'll just follow this on to Newark and we can get onto the dual carriageway somewhere up the road.'

As they rode on, street lights started lining the road more regularly. The road was still curvy, but after a mile or so, the void-like darkness from before was behind them and there were scatterings of houses on both sides, along with an actual sidewalk for pedestrians – a true symbol of civilization in rural Lincolnshire. Ahead was a sign that said Thomas Parkin Academy.

'Oh look. A school,' said Ben.

Janie barely heard what he said because her attention was fixed on the tall figure walking just past the sign. A shudder ran through her as the man turned to face them and stuck his arm out, thumb pointed to the sky like a beacon.

Ben saw Janie's blankness and said, 'Hitchhiker. Don't see many of them around, do you?'

They cruised past the jeans and white t-shirt clad tall man, who turned to watch as they passed him by, his face blanketed in darkness.

'No, we're not picking you up, jerkoff! Sorry!' scoffed Ben. Despite making light of the walker, he kept an eye on the side mirror and caught a glimpse of the hitchhiker stumbling into the street as they passed – but instead of dragging himself back to the sidewalk, he started running after them.

Janie looked in the rearview and shouted, 'Is he chasing us?'

Ben's heart sank, but he remained calm for both their sakes. He snickered, 'Yeah, but just keep driving. He's way back there and we're going thirty. That's scary as shit, though.'

They both kept quiet, peeking into the rear and side mirrors every few seconds just to make sure the tall man wasn't somehow back in sight and legging it towards them. After a few more twists and bends, they passed a sign that said WELCOME TO TUXTON.

'Looks like you were right,' said Ben as they passed the sign, stopping at another T-junction not far down the road.

Directly in front of them stood a centuries-old building with THE GOLDSMITH'S ARMS sprawled on the façade in big gold letters and another sign pointing them toward Newark.

Janie's fear of the chasing pedestrian was suddenly overshadowed by an overwhelming feeling of déjà vu. 'We were just here, weren't we?' she asked.

'I don't think so.'

'Yeah. Yeah we were. You were sleeping. This must be the same pub. I remember seeing it like ten minutes ago.'

Ben snickered. 'You're losing it, babe.'

She turned her head, looked him dead in the eyes and said, 'Don't do that, Ben. I swear we were just here.' She rarely took his quips seriously, but this one went to the heart.

'Well what do you want me to do? The sign says left to Newark, so go left.'

She was getting fed up, not with him entirely, but with the whole situation. 'I went left last time and ended up on that dark stretch of road with fields on both sides.'

'Are you sure?'

She squinted her eyes and tilted her head in a don't-be-stupid sort of way. 'Yes, Ben. I'm sure.'

'Just go left again. Let's see what happens,' said Ben.

He was half-tempted to get Janie even more riled up by joking that the tall man was behind them again, but he decided against it and, instead, kept quiet as they turned left. They passed Tuxton's post office, corner shop and several realtor offices before passing through the town's residential area.

'I swear I passed all this while you were asleep. I know it,' said Janie, as Ben struggled to not say a word.

They drove on, past a long strip of box-shaped bungalows, each with its own miniature gated garden at the front, and, within minutes, he knew Janie was right. They were driving down the same dark abyss of rural road they were on when he woke up ten minutes ago.

He knew it was coming, and he was right. 'Told you so,' said Janie.

Ben ignored her and kept quiet, until he noticed the lack of street lights ahead and the white road sign from before creeping its way towards them again – ORIN SLEW – screaming at them from the top of it.

'What the fuck?' blurted Ben as they came to a stop in front of the sign, the reflection of their headlights beaming back at them from the ominous metallic square.

'You're joking, right? How is this even possible?' he asked.

Voice shaking, Janie replied, 'I – I told you … Right again, towards Newark?'

'I guess,' he said, so she gently pressed the accelerator down and turned.

A mile of curved road once again took them away from pitch black farmland and back into society. As the car sped along at a quicker pace than before, the uneasy feeling of familiarity that filled Ben and Janie worsened as the sign touting Thomas Parkin Academy once again approached.

Ben glanced over at Janie and noted the expressionless look on her face as she focused all her attention on the road ahead, her eyes shooting from left to right, looking for the tall hitchhiker. Despite the outrageous circumstances, they were both partially put at ease as they passed the school and saw no sign of him. Janie's foot got a bit heavier, and before they knew it, they passed the same unwelcoming WELCOME TO TUXTON sign from before as The Goldsmith's Arms entered into sight once again.

Janie stopped at the intersection in front of the pub, just as before. Eyes fixed ahead, she asked, 'What now?'

Ben's humor had been abandoned in this same spot ten minutes ago. All he could come out with was a solemn, 'Try right this time, I guess.'

Without question, Janie turned right despite heading away from the direction they should have been going. Both of them breathed a sigh of relief, though, when the buildings passing alongside them were different to the ones before. This time, a library, police station and bank, among other shops and businesses, whizzed by as Janie put the pedal to the metal in hopes of getting home to their soft, warm bed sooner than later.

A quarter mile on, they entered a similar residential area to the one they had driven through during their first lap through Tuxton. Small houses with even smaller gardens at the front filled both sides of the road until the modern day huts were mere dots in the rearview as they entered a strikingly similar stretch of rural road surrounded by blackened emptiness – and then they both saw it ahead.

As the street lights became sparser, a lone white sign at the end of the road came into view. They both remained hopeful that this one didn't flaunt the menacing graffiti of the other, but hope as they did, ORIN SLEW radiated from the same exact spot as before – this time glowing slightly.

'What – the – fuck?' asked Ben. 'What the fuck is happening and where the FUCK are we?' He was hoping for an answer, but didn't get one. He looked beside him and saw Janie's complexion had become as white as the sign in front

of them, mouth opened in fear and tears trickling down her cheeks. Not good, he thought. 'Babe?' he whispered. No response except for a blink. 'Janie? Hey, snap out of it.' He clicked his fingers in front of her face and, after a second, she came back. He cleared the tears from her cheek and asked, 'Do you want me to drive?'

Still partially out of it, she answered, 'Umm. Uhh, yeah. Yeah,' and brought the car to a stop.

'Okay, no problem,' he said, unbuckling his seat belt. No movement from Janie, though. He unclicked her belt and uttered, 'Let's move, though. This place gives me the creeps.' Nothing from her again, so he gave her a shake and shouted, 'NOW!'

This gave Janie the jolt she needed.

'I'll run around to your side. You just shuffle over,' he said. Ben bolted out the passenger side door and shut it as Janie scooched to the left. He got to the driver's side and yanked the handle. The door didn't open. He gave it four or five more pulls in a row. Still nothing. 'SHIT!' he yelled, noticing the tiny red light lit on the padlock inscribed button at the centre of the dashboard.

Janie had turned the central locking system on earlier when they were stuck at a stoplight in an unsavory part of Manchester, securing the car's doors on the outside.

He slammed open palms on the window, but Janie was slipping again. 'Babe? Snap out of it and press the button, please!'

No response.

Not knowing what to do, he scanned the area, looking for a solution. Instead, his heart skipped a beat and his stomach tightened in terror as, in the distance, he saw the hitchhiker from before sprinting towards the car. Adrenaline coursed through Ben's veins as he slammed clenched fists on the door, screaming at the top of his lungs, 'JANIE! UNLOCK THE FUCKING DOOR NOW!!!'

She blinked and snapped out of her stupor, looking at her husband with placid confusion as he relentlessly yanked the door handle.

He screamed again, 'UNLOCK THE DOOR!'

The tall man was close now. So close that the car's tail lights shined a red hue onto him, making the hitchhiker look almost demonic.

Realizing the panic radiating from her husband, Janie pressed the central locking button. The deep, thudding click of automatic car doors unlocking were a godsend to Ben's ears as he swung the driver's side door open and forced the emergency brake off.

He looked in the rearview and, to his terror, the tall man was mere feet from the car, seemingly glowing red now from the brake light Ben had just engaged by stepping on the pedal. Before setting off, instinct kicked in and Ben pressed the central locking button just as the running man yanked Janie's handle. She shrieked in terror as the handle clicked and the door swung open. Ben was too slow.

A forceful hand gripped Janie's shoulder, but luckily she'd buckled herself in and couldn't be pulled out of the car.

Ben cut the wheel to the left and slammed the accelerator down as Janie screamed bloody murder. This forced the passenger door to slam shut on the tall man's arm, weakening his grip so that he lost hold of Janie.

The car sped off, spraying a haze of dust and dirt behind it.

Glancing in the rearview, now yards away from the sign, Ben could see the silhouette of the hitchhiker staggering, holding his arm but still sprinting towards the car. Foot pressed hard against the pedal, the car reached 60 miles per hour in seconds, leaving the tall man far behind.

'What the fuck is happening? Are you all right?' he asked Janie.

Speechless, she gasped, 'I … I don't know.'

Despite turning left instead of right at the ORIN SLEW sign, Thomas Parkin Academy was fast approaching yet again.

'It…it can't be,' said Ben. He wasn't referring to the fact that they'd be passing the school for a third time, despite turning away from it back at the sign. No, he was referencing the fact that standing directly in front of them, in the centre of the road, was the tall man.

Arm mangled at his side, he started running at the car again.

'Wh…what should I do?' he asked Janie.

'I—I don't know.' Then, filled with a sudden burst of confidence, she said, 'Run the bastard down.'

That was all Ben needed to hear, so he slammed his foot down again and dashed head on towards the hitchhiker.

At the last second, though, the tall man bound forward into the air like a bullet, smashing through the windshield. He hung onto the steering wheel with his healthy arm, swaying left and right as the car swerved down the road back towards the WELCOME TO TUXTON sign.

One hand clenched onto the steering wheel, Ben drove his other fist into the tall man's face. Not having any effect, Ben decided to play dirty and poked his fingers into the hitchhiker's eyes, which had a hint of red emanating from them. To his horror, he didn't feel an ooze or puncture following the poke – just nothingness. 'Do something!' he shouted at Janie.

She tried beating at the tall man's hand, which was wrapped around the steering wheel, but to no avail. She gave up and, instead, yanked the emergency brake up, sending the car to a wavy halt as the tall man was flung several yards forward into the road.

Without thinking twice, Ben pushed the emergency brake back down and slammed on the gas pedal, shouting in rage and terror. He lined the driver's side tires up with the downed hitchhiker's head and braced himself. The impact of the first tire sent Ben and Janie up off their seats – but there was no second bump. Confused, Ben hit the brakes and shot a glance into the rearview, hoping to see the hitchhiker's splayed skull and lifeless body in the road behind. Hopes are different to expectations, though, and this time, Ben's expectations were right on the money: the hitchhiker was gone and there wasn't a single remnant of his presence. 'What the …' Ben started, but Janie quickly interrupted.

'Ben, look. The GPS …' she said, pointing at the device which had suddenly found a satellite signal and lit up back to life.

'But that guy – he's …he's gone.'

In an attempt to hold it together so they could make it out of Tuxton, Janie pleaded, 'Ben, the GPS is back on. Let's just get out of here. Please.'

Ben looked like he was fading, like Janie had earlier, and her heart started to drop.

"LEFT TURN AHEAD," instructed the GPS in a robotic, but confident, British brogue.

This was enough to bring Ben back to the present. He blinked and shook his head before noting that the green arrow on the display was directing them to turn left at the Goldsmith's Arms intersection at the centre of town again. Without hesitation, Ben pressed the gas pedal down and cut the wheel towards Newark, past the same post office, corner shop, realtor offices and bungalow-lined area as before. Within minutes, they were back in the black void created by the surrounding farmland. Silence filled the car as a cool breeze blew in from the shattered windshield. And then they saw it for the fourth time. The same white road sign from before, but this time, faintly different – no red ORIN SLEW painted across the top. The GPS said to turn right, so Ben followed, speeding in the direction of Thomas Parkin Academy – but to his and Janie's surprise, before they reached the school, they came to a slip road onto the dual carriageway towards Newark. The GPS advised to turn onto it, and they did.

Despite the smashed windshield, Ben didn't stop driving.

CORPSE ON A GURNEY

By Kirill Ilukhin

He fell down in front of me like a bag full of rotting peaches. The realisation of what had happened didn't hit me immediately, but the understanding of the consequences got to me almost instantly. Illogical, right? Usually, it's the other way around. First you do stupid things, then you're afraid, and then you experience regret for your actions. It worked a little differently in my case.

The first thing I noticed was the smell. What was it? I sniffed. The smell of burnt people? No, I wasn't used to that. Maybe the smell of the now-dead guy, which had been distinctive to him during his lifetime? No, definitely not that. Oh, gunpowder. That was it. White, barely visible smoke rose into the air from a single shot. It fascinated me far more than the ringing in my ears.

The first thing I heard was the cry of the nurse, crouching in the corner of the ward. No idea what her name was, although we talked almost every shift. Nurses didn't care much for the likes of me. They never attached any importance to our existence. But they endured us, and sometimes even smiled. After what had happened today, the nurse would never smile at me again. Even if I moved the revolver from pointing at the corpse, to her. People at gunpoint tended to do everything the person with the weapon said, but today was different.

I killed a man, and I will most likely be declared a hero for it.

But first things first. It was 12 o'clock, and I'd just started my shift. I jumped in the front seat of the ambulance. Instead of greeting Harry, I just nodded at him. Harry nodded too, and started the engine. Somewhere in the back our newbie was whingeing about something. I had decided not to memorise his name until he had proved himself. If you think being a male nurse in the emergency room is like being a doctor, you are mistaken. Yes, we have some medical knowledge, we have experience in intensive care patients in "difficult field conditions", so to speak, but the life of doctors in their offices is more fun and far cleaner than ours. For the most part, we are committed to reanimating the homeless and drinkers on the streets that have miscalculated their evening or morning dose. Doesn't sound nice, does it? The reality is even worse.

Especially for me. I had never liked people, even when I was a child. Well, I was very fond of certain specific people but, watching the news and looking at the faces of politicians, spreading smiles across their fat faces, saying how they were going to raise taxes for those who didn't have much anyway, I hated humanity with all my soul. Hated the whites, because they considered themselves to be the most important in the world; hated the blacks, for doing nothing and living off benefits; hated the Asians for creating a monopolistic market and producing all the goods; the Christians because they were thieves and paedophiles, who had never even opened their own Bible; the Muslims because they killed for an imaginary spirit invented centuries ago. Yes, I hated almost all possible groups of people, and thinking about them made me furious.

My wife left a year ago. I could have said to myself, "Dude, it happens, pull yourself together", but there was one reason why I couldn't. That was my second wife and the second one who had left me. I hadn't lamented much after the first one, Betty. We simply hadn't agreed on things, grown apart; it happens. But when Anna left me, I had realised that I alone was to blame. So a year ago, I had added myself to the list of all those I hated.

And now I'm once again rushing to perform CPR on a homeless guy soaked in alcohol and lice. My job, as I said, wasn't like a doctor's. You brush your teeth, when going to the doctor, and might even take a shower with some luck. My "patients" most likely had finished someone else's half-digested and rejected-through-the-mouth croissant for breakfast. And it's good that it's half-digested because, as a rule, my guys don't have any teeth.

Today's homeless had his teeth in place, but he wasn't breathing anymore. The newbie began to fill out the paperwork, Harry didn't even get out of the vehicle, and I took up my duties. I tried to massage his heart right there, on the spot where they had found this tramp (if only you could smell the aroma of his "home" mixed with the smell of river), but I barely even touched the body when he grabbed my arm and opened his eyes. I jumped back, but instantly pulled myself together. It must be that his heart had begun to beat, and I hadn't noticed. Harry put the radio down, giving the all-clear to the coroner, and we began shipping the homeless guy into the ambulance. All the way he didn't move, but his eyes opened and closed repeatedly. His pupils weren't reacting to light and his pulse wasn't palpable. We call these guys lucky. They have one foot in the grave, but the body just doesn't want to die. Now, we'll bring him to the hospital, the surgeons will work their magic and it may give him a couple of days, but the result will be the same as in thousands of similar cases. Homeless people kill their bodies every day, and we spend time and effort to give them an extra five minutes of existence.

By the time we got Lucky to the hospital, his eyes had stopped twitching. He just stared at the ceiling with a glassy look, as if he were dead. But when we unloaded him from the vehicle, his fingers clenched into fists, and it wasn't like the kind of cramps that can happen after death. His knuckles turned white and black blood flowed from the torn skin on his palms. The newbie, watching it, threw up, which did not cheer me up at all.

Then I raised my head and looked around. There were far too many ambulances in our parking lot. Most of them were not from our district either. People were running around with gurneys at breakneck speeds. There were people with second, third and even fourth degree burns on the gurneys, covered in vesicles and bullae, like rappers in bling. Thermal burns, as far as I could tell, didn't promise anything good for these people. I cheered up a bit, but then remembered that I would be just like the others, forced to clean up this whole mess. Harry, who had time to talk to some of the other nurses, ran up to me and said that a nuclear plant outside the city had exploded. The damage was minimal, there was no threat to the environment, but fifty people would certainly not show up to work tomorrow. We were the nearest hospital capable of admitting all the patients and they were all coming to us. And once we processed our Lucky, we'd be sent off for a new party of "crisps". I gritted my teeth, but said nothing. Another department head hadn't followed safety procedures, another graduate with a degree had no doubt mixed up wires and data, or a worker spilled coffee on the controls, and this was the result – dozens of people baked for a party.

Squeezing between gurneys of people waiting for their turn, and between drips with painkillers, we drove Lucky to find a safe place for him somewhere. After all, the man was on the verge of death, and may have actually been there a couple of times while we were transporting him.

Gurneys with burn victims were scattered everywhere: in the wards, the aisles, even in some of the offices. Moaning could be heard all around and I could smell burnt meat, along with a rotten taste in my mouth. Some of them were probably dead, but it was quite difficult to determine without at least checking the pulse. 'Knock-knock', I said, unceremoniously rolling Lucky into one of the wards that had its doors open. I could tell that the nurse who was there wanted to say that space had run out, but she was apparently too tired to argue. She took the clipboard and approached me to admit my patient. Here is where the fun began.

When the nurse got closer to the gurney, Lucky instantly came to life, so to speak. He growled and shot up; his eyes reflected anything but friendliness. For someone who'd just come to, he remarkably quick as he jumped up and attacked the nurse, nearly breaking her wrist with his sinewy gorilla hands. I barely had time to leap in and put an arm between them. Holding so, I began to chant a soothing mantra, which we had been taught for using when dealing with violent patients and drug addicts. But Lucky wasn't listening; he snarled into the nurse's face and she screamed like an alarm with a broken switch. Just as suddenly, he stopped attacking her, released her hands and looked at me. In his eyes I read all of his desires and aspirations, dark to the very core.

The person in front of me was not living, and definitely not dead.

I pushed him away with all the strength I could muster and he fell near the wall, overturning the gurney. As he was getting up, I replayed all the plots about the walking dead in my head - Brooks, Romero, King, Kirkman and many other wonderful individuals who knew a lot about how to bring pain and suffering to mankind.

Their stories were alike and, at the same time, not. Some didn't bother with what had caused the rising dead, but there were also those who gave a little more sense of what was happening. Religion: the dead have risen to punish humanity. Science: someone invented a deadly virus and now the dead were trampling the land of the living. Contagion: rabid monkey bites someone and it begins. Then there were stories about radiation.

Looks like my Lucky had decided to take a dip in the river just after the nuclear accident occurred. We'll probably never know exactly what had spilled and where. It doesn't really matter now. I was trying to figure out what to do with this "almost dead" next. Perhaps no one but Brooks had given clear tips on what to do if you are faced with a zombie who really wants to eat your face. Everyone usually describes the events as if zombies suddenly become the norm of life, relying on the fact that people just adapt to everything, even if it involves a cow, carried by a hurricane, flying into a window.

You'd be surprised, if you think about. You never get a person in zombie literature saying they can completely destroy the virus that is raising corpses from their graves, and then goes on to save mankind. No, that's not how zombie stories work. No one will read a book about an evil scientist developing a vaccine for the undead for six hundred pages and finally saying: "Well, that didn't work, I'll try another time." Nobody wants to watch a movie where some guy kills the undead "patient zero" in the first ten minutes of the zombie uprising, and the rest of the film he's lauded as a hero. Why not? Because it's too boring. You read about zombies, watch movies about them, play games about zombies, only to see and feel how bad humanity is as it writhes in agony and the undead prey on the remaining populace. This kind of plot doesn't fly without a good dark apocalypse.

But, in my case, the plot was the worst possible, though I didn't know it yet. I've mentioned the guy who killed "patient zero" at the beginning of the movie ... I became that guy. I always carried a weapon, though it was forbidden. I didn't trust TASERs and, while on duty, I visited places where normal people should not set foot. I had to talk to people who couldn't care less that you're working on the ambulance and helping those in need. They just want some money, and don't mind stick a knife into someone's kidneys to get it. When I first started working on the ambulance, I hadn't believed those tales, until I personally stumbled across such types. They're not easily frightened by any TASER or club, especially if they gather in groups of more than one. But a small revolver was an entirely different matter. Pointed at the head, it can dissuade even the worst junkie from taking what's not his.

It was this baby that I pulled out when the undead chap attacked me again. The sound of the shot thundered through the entire hospital, and just as instantly went quiet. It seemed even those who were dying from burns began to moan not so loudly. Or was it just that I had gone temporarily deaf, because I also missed the nurse's screams at first. Lucky fell in exactly the place where, a moment ago, he'd been trying to get up. I stood staring at him, the chill up my spine intensifying with every minute.

I was scared; I had fired; I had just made the biggest mistake of my life.

Today, right now, in this very ward, a real zombie apocalypse could have begun. Hundreds of people all around who couldn't have done anything as this random homeless man began to create his large army of undead. All it had required was for me to step aside and give him freedom. Let him have the nurses and Mary, the fat woman from reception. Let him eat Harry for a snack, and Betty and Anna together. Everyone. All the people on the planet. All that I hated would have started to die in that moment, but only if I had not pulled the trigger.

I could have gone to a house in the wilderness and imagined it as a horde of undead destroyed Parliament, gobbled up fat politicians, eat prostitutes on the bridges, drug addicts, homeless people, priests, terrorists, the police. Even if I had become one of them, what was so wrong about that? I would have done the same thing as them but with far greater zeal.

And so the nurse stops screaming. People come into the ward. Doctors, hospital staff, lightly wounded patients. The nurse tells them what happened. They slap me on the back and say I'm a hero, that they will definitely mark this act in my personal file and give me a bonus this month.

But I'm only half-listening. I've just shot my dream and saved the world I want to destroy. The day simply could not have gone worse.

Tears stream down my cheeks.

LE MAUVAIS PAS

By Ian McCawley

I sink down deeper now. Faster, with the weight of the day. I try to kick, but I'm too tired. Like grasping talons, tendrils of bladderwrack rise from the seabed, intent on dragging me down the steep harbour shelf.

I hear the rush of trapped oxygen molecules and the pounding pulse in my ears. Lungs screaming to expel the deadly carbon dioxide, brain urging me to hold my breath. Despite the dusk and depth there remains a half-light, and my eyes settle on the bobbing hull of a rowing boat yards to my right. An oar slaps limply against the side of the vessel, a dull thud just audible above the thrumming of my heartbeat. I push myself away from the shore, a final clutch at this lifeline. Momentum takes me towards the wooden pole and I grasp, a gasp escaping me.

Eoin sets down the glass. The thump of its base on the uncovered table jolts me out of my waking nightmare. No question, no quizzical looks. I'm grateful for that at least.

'They don't call it Le Mauvais Pas for nothing,' Eoin says. He knows something's up, of course. Paul's not here. Could be that we had merely been arguing again, or that he'd needed to get back to the mainland and sped off for the last ferry once we were back from the ridges. But my silence and stare give away too much, as if I am a man already condemned.

Le Mauvais Pas. The bad step. Perhaps it had wrong-footed both of us the moment I'd pored over the OS map, mesmerised by the clustered contours that suddenly dropped away. An eerie shaft in a narrow mountain ridge. A legendary, lonely place that had captured my imagination. Views that had to be seen. The walkers' blog had sounded like an estate agent's website, unequivocal in its praise of the vertiginous spot.

I realise I haven't untied my walking boots. They have been like lead weights since my scramble down the mountainside. Eoin dries glasses and observes me from behind the bar, its oak surface reflecting the lights gleaming above the optics. The bulbs and the becalmed embers of the fire are the only things scaring off the gloom as evening descends. It's darker in here than it is outside, a perversity of the island's northern latitude.

I move to the window, my back to Eoin, and taste the cool ale for the first time. On better nights I would savour the hoppy flavour of the stout, but tonight it seems loaded with meaning. A stout pair of boots. A stout constitution. Neither had come to Paul's rescue on the barren plateau half a mile above us.

My solemn expression is reflected in the pane that looks out onto the deserted harbour. I look gaunt tonight, remarkably like Paul. My cheeks are pinched and weary, decorated by the beginnings of scratchy stubble. Chores done, Eoin moves over to join me, sitting in the window seat. With the failing light at his back, he cuts a bulky silhouette against the bobbing fishing boats behind him. He's fetched a whisky glass and settles into the chair's tatty cushions, brushing a hand over his thick beard. I remain silent. His own tone is neutral, unaccusing. 'Come on then, Richard. What happened up there?'

No matter what the season, we'd always savoured the promise of a few hours in the hills. City life was humdrum and hiking made us feel closer to nature, like it had when we were kids. Paul was a bit quieter than normal. I put it down to the dodgy stomach he'd complained of last night. As we pulled on our boots, I gazed excitedly up at the mountains, already on the lookout for deer or golden eagles. They were nesting again close to this northern coast and, with few other passers-by to disturb their brood in a remote part of the island, I thought we might catch a glimpse.

We stepped off the shore road, passing along a rocky track that soon led on to soft turf. The path wound its way past the solemn site of the island's cemetery on the left. To our right was the cricket pitch, which seemed an incongruous location, just over the way from the mossy tombstones. My imagination ran riot; hit the ball out of the ground and you'd be in danger of wreaking eternal havoc. I daydreamed of skeletons and spectres doing battle between the stumps: a Danse Macabre at the dusty wicket. It was a picturesque place to play a match, under the gaze of mountains that rose all around. The pitch and the graveyard made uneasy companions though, and I shivered as we walked by.

Now the track weaved into the bottom of the glen. The land rose away from the shore and gave spectacular views over the firth behind us. Further ahead I saw the long, steep climb into dense pines. It seemed a shame we'd eventually leave the sunny but cooler air of the valley to be encased by the trees. The oppressive canopy would create an extra layer of sheen as we sweated from the effort of climbing and lugging our packs. Still, there was the river to enjoy before then.

Half a mile further on, underneath the hanging valleys glowering above, we tarried to top up water bottles and adjust boots. I'd been aware of Paul's near-silence all the way up from the coast road. The odd grunt here and there, an acknowledgment of my remarks about nature's spectacle and the wonder of the day around us. Aside from that he was sullen. Now, as we both snapped off a finger of biscuit by the burn, all his dammed thoughts came flooding out.

'You've never really been there for me, you know.' His voice was flat, but there was a simmering heat beneath the words, bubbling away like the eddies of the river as they whirled and swept around the smooth stones of the ford ahead of us.

I turned to face him. If he was harbouring resentment, I couldn't think why. 'I don't know what-'

Paul got to his feet. He did it so abruptly that, for a moment, I thought he was going to lose his balance and splash down into the shallows. Instead he rocked on his heels, then placed his right foot on the side of a boulder jutting out above me. His features were darkened by the effect of standing with the sun at his back. His unruly, dark blonde hair and angular cheekbones made him resemble a young Clint Eastwood as he squinted down at me from his superior position. I knew he was intent on staking a claim to some moral high ground. He said, 'The will, Richard. You know full well.'

I racked my brains. Then it dawned on me: Dad had mentioned something a while ago about solicitors and "eleventh-hour changes". He was well on the way to his final curtain and I had put his ramblings down to dementia. I began to wish I'd paid more attention. I'd suspected he and Paul had argued but I was busy with work at the time. Paul's capacity for petty feuds and spite were well-trodden family byways; God knows the two of us had spat some teeth at each other over the years, but his truck was usually with Dad. I'd long since decided not to mediate - they could fight their own battles. More often than not the rows were forgotten and forgiven, though that did little to stop Paul reoffending. Now, with Dad gone, it seemed like Paul's poor-me was newly focussed on yours truly.

'You're wrong, bro,' I answered, shielding my eyes from the sun. I was trying to keep it light, but Dad's revelations were coming back to haunt me. I felt like I'd colluded, known all along that the inheritance had been changed in my favour.

'Am I really?' he snarled, and fixed me with a steely glare. It was a look I had got used to as we grew up, but had never been scared of. Paul was in the short-fuse club, but it took a lot to get me going. 'How do I know you weren't round there, in Dad's ear as usual?' He was breathing hard, despite not breaking sweat over the last mile.

I sighed, trying to soothe him. 'Even if Dad had spoken to me, why would I have listened? You two might have been at each other's throats, but not me and you, Paul. Besides, Mum's still here. There's time to change things. And if that's not possible, you can have your fair share of whatever I get.'

As rapidly as the storm clouds around Paul's head gathered, they cleared again. He paused. His breathing slowed. He chuckled, almost to himself, and put the last bit of biscuit into his mouth, then shook his head and smiled. 'All right. Why let my mood swings spoil a good day? We can deal with this properly later.' He gestured towards the ford, waiting for me to cross. I was still feeling quite cautious, uneasy after our exchange. He sighed, rolled his eyes, then heaved on his pack. Seconds later he'd leapt across two big stones into the middle of the burn. I followed, and we rejoined the path on the other side where the ground was boggier.

I wouldn't say our silence was companionable as we trudged on, but it beat the tension of before. Soon the track left the marshy grass by the river and began to climb. As we trudged along the curved spine of a hummock, the full extent of the mountainside above us reared into view: the thick copse between here and the ridge, and atop it the foreboding fractures we'd come to conquer. Le Mauvais Pas, a great crack spearing down into the ground like the root of a tooth.

Up we climbed. I was glad the sky had remained clear

and the air was still. The mountains jagged a thousand feet further into the air. Just the gentlest breeze could whip up a thin curl of cloud into a broiling fog, leaving the rambler stranded.

My brother seemed just as anxious to get to the top. The forest stood in our way and, when we reached the treeline, he plunged straight into its green shroud. We'd climbed the best part of a thousand feet and there was a rudimentary bench just outside the first rank of firs. It was an ideal place to stop, catch our breath, rub down a blister or two and gaze back over the sun-soaked shore. Paul though, had other things on his mind.

'Hold on a sec, Richard.' Eoin rolls the Rs in my name in that peculiarly beautiful way that belongs to the Scots. 'I need a top-up.' He levers himself out of the chair and wanders stiffly back to the bar. His gout has evidently got worse but he isn't letting it stop him tonight. Hardly surprising, given the tone I've used to tell my tale. I'm trying to control my shock and keep my voice down, and it's making me talk more gruffly than normal.

There's a figure; over the road, where the evening is falling fast against the backdrop of the mill-pond firth, I can swear I see a walker standing there, one foot planted in front of the other. Bedraggled, crooked. Something about him, telegraphing pain. I step nearer the window for a closer look, but a vehicle travelling south passes by and then nothing is there.

Eoin is shuffling back to his seat. He looks as if he's read my mind and peers out into the strange ochre light. 'Storm brewing, son.' He tuts, like the onset of thunder is going to ruin a planned evening of careless festivities. 'Now, where were you?'

Right here, I think to myself. For a few moments more though, my mind is across the road, searching for whoever

– or whatever – was standing there. There's a bubbling in my stomach. I drink deep from my half-empty glass, hoping to clear the acid while I confess the rest.

The way through the forest was more a trampoline than a path. A thick bed of springy pine needles at my feet, a dense sense of foreboding above my head. I felt hemmed in. Paul was setting a fine pace in front but it was like something was dragging behind us up the hill. I sensed the demons swirling in his mind weren't done.

When he was younger, Paul had been obsessive. First, football. There wasn't a City player from the initial 12 years of his life whose inside leg measurement he didn't know. Next, inevitably, came girls. Or one in particular: Zoe Wood. He finally wore her down when they were 18, but she broke his heart at 19. After that, he struggled with relationships.

More recently he'd got into swimming. He was good at it. He spent a lot of time on his own in the water and I'd begun to wonder if it was unhealthy. He'd go to the pool morning and evening, putting off other things – like socialising and finding a proper job – and had become scrawny. I believed it was his own answer to my skills as a climber, more envy he'd never come to grips with. They were his own keen interests, most people would say. I knew differently; I'd seen it all before. I could almost hear the flies buzzing in his head. I wondered if he'd taken his tablets.

The path doglegged and the woods got darker. We'd been under the canopy for an hour and I was starting to pine for fresh air. It was static in here and sweat dappled my forehead. Paul was a good fifty yards away, not looking back, but I felt he was testing me, daring me to catch up with him as he stretched ahead into the gloom. I kept my distance instead, trying to tune into the distractions of the flora and fauna.

Another incline and I'd lost him among the gathering shadows. Suddenly the path ducked out under the high treeline, and finally I was out on the fell. I hadn't realised how high we'd climbed – we must have been well over two thousand feet by then, though it was hard to tell with the forest obscuring the valley floor. There was still some way to go but we were within striking distance of Le Mauvais Pas. Sure enough, as we neared the island's ceiling, the first wisps of cloud began to drift down the hillside. I looked nervously towards the spill of scree that led up to the vertical fissure and wondered whether we were doing the right thing.

Where was Paul? He couldn't possibly have got the legs on me to be out of sight. In which case, I thought, he must be among the boulders strewn around the slope, the roche moutonnée offering plenty of places to lie low.

I looked ahead again, feeling the pull of the shattered ridge. There was no path down the sheer mountainside, so unless I wanted an immediate trudge back through the forest, the only way was up. I shrugged off my anxiety about Paul, assuming he'd show up soon enough. It was time to do what we'd come here for.

The 200-foot route was a thigh-busting scramble, but needed no rope. The rocks below the summit were broken and treacherous but, thanks to my climbing skills, it caused me no real hardship. The real drama met me at the top. The ridge was a thin ribbon, hovering no more than a handful of feet wide with sheer drops on both sides. If that wasn't risky enough, the path was punctuated to my left by the yawning gap of Le Mauvais Pas. Two metres wide, a chasm ending in the rubble one hundred feet below, shattered spikes of rock reaching up to spear the unlucky climber. Deadly but so, so tempting. If there is a gap anywhere else in the world like that which has so silently, yet strongly, beckoned a leap of faith, I don't know it. The pull across to the eastern side, otherwise inaccessible, is magnetic, but the two metres are just wide enough to risk limb and life. What's more, if you chance it, the only way down the mountain is to leap back again. What fool would do that?

'Chaos theory,' Paul whispered over my shoulder, and I jumped. I was so in awe standing on the edge of the ravine that I hadn't noticed him creeping up behind me. He too must have climbed quickly; quicker than I'd given him credit for.

'Crikey Paul, I nearly fell down there,' I said, chuckling nervously.

There was that glare again. This time though, there was something more sinister behind his eyes, and it was accompanied by a twitch in his right eyelid. I suddenly felt very alone on this barren crest, sweating in the sun, the lightest of breezes whistling around the hollows. No, not alone - scared.

'Climber aren't you?'

Here we go again, I thought wearily, but not without a glance at the danger all around us.

'More polished, the one with the charm, sailing through life. I'm not finished by a long chalk. And you're not getting away with it.'

He paced up and down, then began to walk around me in tight circles. I heard agitation in his breath but his footsteps somehow found safety despite our precarious position. Half of me was terrified he'd slip and plummet from the ridge, while the other half was desperate to escape the madman clearly rising up within him.

He stopped. His face was no more than a yard away, snarling into mine, and I instinctively edged backwards. I had turned on the spot to face him while he moved and I realised with dismay that Le Mauvais Pas gaped behind me. My voice low I said, 'Paul – what the hell's got into you? Stop it, stop it now.'

'No way, no chance,' he snarled, creeping forward. 'For once in my life I've got you exactly where I want you. A tragic accident, a mother in mourning and a clear path for me. It shouldn't be too hard to get that money once you're out of the picture.'

I knew what I had to do. I was close enough now. I prayed, jumped and turned in one fluid movement. I made it and felt a surge of adrenaline.

I spun just in time to catch sight of the horror on Paul's face. He'd dived after me but misjudged the crack, which seemed somehow wider from this side. He caught himself briefly on the ledge, the top half of his face visible for a long moment. That narrow stare had turned into imploring, wide eyes. Yet I didn't move. And he dropped.

My voice is hoarse with the shock of the story flooding out. I recount the last part of my nightmare hike. Eoin listens as I convince him – or is it myself? – that of course I cared. Paul had wanted to harm me, but he was my brother. I had shouted his name as I scrambled down the mountain to where the deadly crack spewed out the boulders. It had been to no avail. I could see his broken body, motionless at the foot of the chasm, but I just couldn't reach him. So I made my way home.

'During that hour or two, however long it took me to reach the road, something changed.' I breathe quicker, bile rising in my throat. 'I realised, I knew not only that it was too late, but I didn't regret it either.'

I sit back, not looking at Eoin, staring instead at the stained varnish of the table as I empty the pint glass. I'd barely noticed, almost hypnotised by my own voice, but Eoin has lit one of his small cigars. He flicks off the ash and folds his arms. Pursing his lips, he says, 'Richard, I need to make some calls. You'd better sit here.'

I wait, fetching breaths in ragged gasps. Eoin stands and, as he walks past, he pats me gently on the shoulder. He leaves the room, closing the door quietly. I'm here alone with misery and uncertainty. Suddenly the snug pub feels more like a claustrophobic cocoon. I need to get out.

The evening air is mercifully cool and the road is quiet. The heat of the day, and the hustle and bustle of hikers and tourists, is gone. I stand for a while as the last of the sun's rays disappear over the moors on the other side of the bay.

I could have helped him yet I had left. What had I thought he would do to me, bashed up among the rocks? Panic had driven me down the hillside. Now it's settling around me like a shroud of guilt.

There's a scraping noise; shoes on concrete. I turn, and my heart leaps. Paul's standing there, but it's not Paul. His clothes all right, and his frame. His cheeks are shredded though, the left eye a horrific, gluey sphere exposed between lifted lids. The right eye is gone. I try to speak, but nothing comes out. Paul is ambling towards me, bloodied palms spread by his sides. What's left of his face is pitted with flecks of rubble. His sneer says it all, and I understand his intentions. One step back in fear is too far. I plunge.

Bobbing up, gasping, I realise the flat surface is instead a churning tide, waves whipped by a growing gale as Eoin's storm arrives at the wrong moment. Instinct urges me to grasp for the shore and my feet desperately seek purchase on the submerged slipway. Though Paul is nowhere in sight, I dread escaping the swell only for him to finish the job. Indecision upon me, I slide back into the water, shocked how deep it is this close to the road, and how very cold. I'm pulled under.

With bitter irony, the thought strikes me that our talents were gifted the wrong way round, unable to save us on this day. Me the climber, him the swimmer; as above, so below. The oar evades my grasp, and soon our own bad steps will reunite us in eternity.

SOVEREIGN

By Anna Milon

'Will you give me a coin?' An unlikely address grates on his ears. Swedes may be friendly folk, but for a child to approach a stranger in the streets of Stockholm is rare enough. Still, a lifetime of injected politeness makes him turn around.

'Why would you need a coin?' The girl-child looks nothing like an urchin. Rather, a curious offspring of well-to-do parents. Children like her handle money from an early age, do not fall ill with measles or flu; are clean, goodly, suitable …

'Mommy said, the tooth fairy will come and put a coin under my pillow when I'm asleep. But she must have forgotten.' She is a plan yet to be mediated; a veiny blueprint of "woman", nominal. The minimalist a la mode features are shaded by a stiff crepe ribbon threaded through unruly hair.

'Do I look like a tooth fairy?' To apply time-lapse now and raise her from the sheltered shell-hood is … not tempting; far too many dull consonants to do her justice; exhaustive, like the flame choked upon itself before it is aspark with self-importance – he shivers, caught in the gasp of chill from the harbour, and a half-remembered past: the plastic surgeons that leeched his bank accounts in that "before" time.

'No, but I like you. I would want to marry someone like you.' It is a small naïve palm reaching. It suddenly is … the sun.

The radio screeched nervously. 'Krrr … eastern door … krr … ne down.'

'Jan, what the hell is going on in there?! Hello?' Assistant inspector Thorsvik slid off the police frequency, allowing himself some pathos once no one could hear. 'Sod this - I'm going in.'

The door had been prudently swept off its hinges by the SWAT team, but the sizeable mansion, like a coy mistress, defied being searched from top to bottom. Keeping his ears perked, Thorsvik skipped the two lower floors and headed straight up the curvaceous staircase. The air smelled clean and dry.

'How hard could it be to get a nice clear tip-off,' the policeman mused, 'without having to run around the premises like a dog chasing shadows, only to discover it was the wrong house to begin with?' The doors creaked as soon as he touched them, one by one, opening up into clean, tidy rooms. No grisly ropes, manacles or any such unsavoury ware associated with a serial abductor.

Creak, creak, snap.

No, it was definitely the wrong house. Thorsvik almost jumped as he peeked into the next room. He might have missed it altogether, lulled into complacency by the doors. Not the room; the person in the room. A woman in lacquered shoes. She smiled at Thorsvik.

He scrambled for the radio on his belt with sweaty fingers.

'Jan, I've got a victim. Female, 'bout 20. No, 15. The hell should I know! The bastard must've left her here when he scrambled. Send me someone, yeah.' Having blurted out the request, Thorsvik tried to steady his voice.

'It's all going to be fine, miss. You're safe. You're going to be fine.'

The female's smile broadened, her shoes squeaking leathery. Did you bring me a coin?

Thorsvik paced the small interrogation room – obligations buffeted him around like rough spring winds. With the trail growing cold, this girl was the police's only connection to the criminal. Why were the likes of him never given names, even fake ones? It was difficult enough to see him as a person as it was. Anywhere was better than where the girl had come from; it excused the cell. She had been detained for questioning, compassion squelched underfoot like a wizened apple.

'What's your name?'

'He called me Elsinore.'

'And must've dubbed himself Hamlet.' Thorsvik chuckled mirthlessly, remembering the name of the castle in the play.

'No. Every fortress needs a dragon.'

A blackberry briar grows from a girl's pelvis. This is fertile soil; their moon-garden. The Dragon kneels, parts the moist turf with his hands and shows Elsinore a skull, clean yellow, lit by the moon. Its mouth is a gap-toothed line no good for kissing. But Elsinore's loveliness, liveliness begs for the dark beady fruit, glistening tongue stained with their juice. They consume in silence.

'...25, 24, 23, 22.' He really should have started from the other end. The assistant detective counted down patiently. The girl was meant to stop him when he reached her age (straightforward questions appeared to go anywhere but forward). Elsinore was silent. Behind her, a psychotherapist assigned to the department shuffled from one foot to another uncomfortably. ' ...8, 7, 6...'

'Stop!' Elsinore raised a narrow hand, palm out. The psychotherapist - Max or something along those lines - rolled his eyes in a long-suffering fashion.

'Just to be clear … your age from the moment of birth.'

'Yes; since the moment of birth. It was six times February 29th. Six.'

Thorsvik scratched his temple and wrote: 24 years old – a

guess. She eyed the writing upside down.

'I am lying to you.'

'What?' It took two attempts to swallow, then to put the pen down (not throw; no, put down, carefully). Fortunately, the intercom bleeped and Thorsvik skulked out of the room.

'*She's been through a lot, that one.*'

Down the corridor, photos and x-rays of her were handed out: pieces of a girl, bracketed by the metal arcs of her bra and the faint smudge of hipbones. There too the delicate void of her abdominal cavity and the coils of gut, like sleepy-headed eels in the shallows – not pregnant, maybe she never woud be. She'd been awfully calm all along. Not drugged; at least nothing they could find. It was better if she stayed with Max for the time being. He seemed like a decent guy even though he'd been around for less than a month.

Elsinore did indeed stay. Quietly, as was her natural state, rolling one creaky shoe from heel to toe. Creak, creak …

Tap. A coin slapped onto the table in front of her: a one Krona piece embossed with a trout, flexed mid-jump. Max wasn't there, but she was not alone. Like the princess in the story – not hungry yet not fed; not clothed, yet not bare. Elsinore rose, flourished, her being surging with recognition of the Dragon leaning over her.

'As you were,' his voice ghosted, compelling her to sit back down. 'Well played.'

His hand swept along the girl's shoulders – a sleek scaly tail slinking discretely into the shirtsleeve. To Elsinore, the words were on a par with rapturous applause; the loudest shouts of "Encore!" from the pit. The Dragon's praise.

His leaving left her unsure whether he was real, but for the touch.

'Mister, why do you never lock doors?'

'Why do you never leave?' The girl is soft and warm, she leans into him, rubs her cheek over his callused palm. In time, he will teach her the entirety of himself, his knowledge. Now, Elsinore is asleep, like the long Scandinavian winter. But it is warm here, hot even. He forces himself down – it is not yet time. She is still not ready.

'What are those: crystal slippers?' The warden, a sow-like inspector with greasy hair eyed Elsinore's shoes with distaste. They were against the rules for detainees; against her un-understanding of beauty.

'Fur-trimmed slippers.' Elsinore interjected quietly, but loudly enough for everyone to notice that her German was as good as her Swedish, without any hint of an accent. The warden was aggressively ignorant. In the original fairy-tale about Cinderella, her shoes were trimmed with fur and were a symbol of the female genitalia, as well as an allegory for sexual awakening.

Thorsvik had only just noticed that the toe and heel of each elegant shoe was covered in short black hairs.

Click. Click. Click. He teaches her to dance. 'Merely imagine you already know how to. Do not be afraid.' Until her feet are rubbed raw. But the Dragon is oblivious to the blistering heat that is causing the fortress walls to wither. And her skin grows no harder as she – again and again – forces her feet to blister and keeps dancing.

Time ticks down as sand trickles – German, English, Latin, watercolours. She wants to learn loving. Not yet. Scabs on her heels heal; thus ends the polar night. Light leeches colour from her skin and his hair.

'Why is eternity not ours?'

'Hours?' The Dragon has forever, whatever he has it for, even when there is no dust from the bricks of this fortress. No path of crumbs to find a way home; no home. Needs must hurry, ere the day see Elsinore unraised, unravished. Today.

Fruit became her tutors over the bleak summer. Then there were none. The detainee rations contained boiled potatoes, wilted greens and meat; all perfectly nourishing, but no fruit. They kept asking Elsinore questions she did not understand the necessity to answer. Words like "violence" and "abuse" sounded harsh, but had no impact outside their acoustic unpleasantness.

People came and went, thrown into relief against her.

'But he killed! Nobody even bothered to do a body-count based on the meagre remains! Girls like you! He's a murderer!' A fleck of spittle bubbled onto the tabletop just left of her arm.

'Not like. They were not suitable. I was.'

The prophetic lisp of Elsinore's sibilants - it suddenly clicked with Thorsvik that her surety was not an act of ignorance, nor the placidity of a sacrificial lamb. Not the kind of woman, whose lips whet with curiosity at the malign, the bestially vulnerable in those creatures – men – they were taught to fear. This one was guileless and effortless in her erectness, exuding the indomitable rectitude of a female in league with a male.

'She won't be on our side unless we tell her to be afraid of him,' he mused over cheap beer. 'After all, we teach our children to fear snakes.'

There is an island park near Stockholm – Skansen, the only one for miles with a real forest. The first time they are spied upon by squirrels; Elsinore is bashful of their oily bead-eyes. The second time she sees water (inches from her face) and breathes it. The third time, the Dragon's talons embrace her through two fickle layers of skin.

Night comes again. Or winter. Every time Elsinore saves a word to say, each time she forgets what begs to be said. She still thinks they have enough.

'They will find you. There is so much of you in me, they sense it.' The coin pricked her palm, sharpened by years of devout polishing. 'They have taken all of me away. Naught remains.'

This was the last of her meagre riches, exposed like bones by the police and doctors and social workers. They knew everything; they smelled her out, word by word. The Dragon embraced her, but his hands fell through emptiness; only sand remained from the fortress. By morning it would be blown away by the wind from the harbour. He had no judgement to pass on the world. Elsinore handed him the coin – one Krona, a trout back broken in mid jump. The last.

But he is real now, standing before her, twisting fingers into his pocket.

'I shall not part with my treasure. Not one single piece.' The edge sinks into her palm when he folds his hand over hers, and presses harder. A drip: first blood. The circle is about to close, but the Dragon is wary to look for another. She is too perfect – unafraid; unpolluted by men, by the ideas of men; only him. The Dragon remembers the faces he wore before, how he was changed, and marvels anew at Elsinore's unaltered state.

He exhales a line of fire against her lips, along the sunken cheek, crossing the wet comet of a tear; re-invoking the comfort of touch that he raised her to cherish. The expanses of them entwine – planes honed, studied, molten and reformed into a unison breath of sheer gratitude, a mutual understanding. Whoever their adversaries might be now, they will catch nothing again. 'I have brought you a bomb.' he murmurs. This is, of course, the only way to stay together.

Elsinore thinks of the fire-flowers their bodies will become. A bomb, a bomb, like the strike of a clock; like a black hole – one part of her ripped at the event horizon, the other enfolded safely in the Dragon's arms. She wonders which one will be real.

He made the detonator many years ago, long before Elsinore. It is old and several moments pass weightlessly – what if it does not work? They will be led out of this room separated, parting red and black, white and blue, the rasp of her shoes and his breathing. But the contraption clicks, jerks against his hand. Everything becomes bright, flooding the snake-dance of voices; husks of emotions as everything condenses, conforms, compounds, combusts into a single, perfect –

ANOTHER SKIN

By Melanie Whipman

I tell them what they want to hear. 'I've got the money.'

Anyone else would have used a transparent bank envelope and a wad of cash, but Dad's given me coins in a little scarlet sack. I hold up the little silk bag and jostle it in the air to disguise the trembling of my hands.

'Princess!'

'Dad?' I peer in the direction of his voice but the room's dark and so choked with cigar smoke I can hardly make him out.

'About time.'

The door sucks itself softly shut behind me and I walk forwards, my feet sticking to the carpet and my throat constricting against the fumes. I love that fuggy pub-smell of stale beer and smoke, but here there's something different, something sickly sweet, metallic and cloying.

They're in the far corner: shadows that morph into men as I approach: four of them sitting around a low table, loosened collars, palmed-up shirtsleeves. There are two more in suits, leaning against the bar. One of the seated guys stabs out his cigar and shunts back his chair.

'I'm out.' He dips his chin at me as he brushes past.

'Princess.' Dad's at the third stage. He's not slurring fully yet but the "r" is slightly furred and his actions are over-controlled. He places his cards face down on the table and holds up the flat of his hand in greeting.

'Car's outside. Why don't you come home, Dad?'

'You going to introduce us, Mike?' The man sitting with

155

his back to me turns and purses out a cloud of Montecristo. 'Hello, princess - I'm Steve.'

'Your money.' I toss him the bag and he snatches it from the air and weighs it in his hand.

'Dad, let's go.'

Dad waves me silent. 'There's enough there for another game … if Mr Skin's happy to let me try and win my money back.'

Steve Skin: the name's appropriate – his sallow face is as pockmarked as a plastic ashtray. I've heard of him; drugs and gambling. And shifting around at the back of my mind there's a tale of betrayal and torture and bolt-cutters.

Steve Skin bares his teeth in a smile. 'Why not? Get her a drink.'

'No thanks.' I try to catch Dad's eye, but he's topping himself up from a bottle of JD. It's pointless, but I try anyway. 'Let's go home.'

'See, just like her mother.' He rolls out a crick in his neck and takes a glug of whisky. 'You go, love. I'll be back in a bit.'

'Fine.'

As I turn to leave, Steve Skin stands up and slides an arm around my shoulders. 'Stay.' Beneath the expensive aftershave and mouthwash I get a whiff of decaying meat. 'To look after your old dad?' His arm's hot and heavy on my shoulder and I can see the moisture gleaming on his mottled skin. He clicks his fingers at the men at the bar. 'Get her a chair and a drink.'

I keep my expression pleasant. 'Sorry, I've got an early start.'

'What d'you do?'

'I teach sewing.'

'Sewing?' He raises his eyebrows. 'Not life and death then.'

'And spinning.'

'Spinning? Spinning yarns? A spin-doctor?'

'I start early.'

'Sorry princess; I insist.' The short, squat, bald one brings across a barstool. Steve Skin fondles the seat. 'Antelope hide. Skinned it myself. Used to be a furrier, did you know that? The skill's in peeling it off, not cutting it. So the hide stays clean.' He shoves out his chest, rolls his shoulders. 'I was the best.'

He puts me in mind of Putin: the same stocky posturing; the feigned affability.

'Most tanners cut the legs off with a meat saw. I prefer bolt-cutters.' His fingers curl into fleshy sausages as they caress the skin. 'This place was a tannery. Accounts for the heat; we dried the hides here.'

I imagine animals splayed on racks. A swirl of nausea curdles my stomach. I should leave. He pats the stool and I hold his eyes for a moment to show I'm not scared. It's the hottest summer in a decade but down here in the basement it's worse than outside. The backs of my knees are pricking, and my jeans are glued to my skin but, as I hoist myself onto the stool, I'm grateful for their covering.

'You'd have thought it would be cool in here, wouldn't you, the Thames just metres away? It's the pipes, they run under the floorboards; keep it cosy.' He drops the pouch onto my lap. 'You hang onto that, princess.' His fingertips needle along my thigh. 'Maybe his luck's going to turn.' He squeezes my knee. 'What's your poison?'

I check my phone. - no reception. 'Soda water.'

He huffs out a laugh and nods to the other guy at the bar.

They play in silence. There's just the soft sliding of the cards and the clink of ice against glass, the creak of a chair, and the occasional slow exhalation of cigar smoke. They signal sticking or folding with an upheld palm or slice of the hand. The third man leaves after fifteen minutes, his brow pleated and damp. He avoids my eyes as he slips past in a waft of BO and whisky.

The second man at the bar brings my soda water. He's thin and dark and slightly hunched. Or maybe just stooped, in the way some of my students are after an adolescent growth spurt, as if he's uncomfortable in his skin. I can't see his face, but I notice the cut and fabric of his suit.: hand stitched, enamel monogrammed buttons. Would have cost a fortune. I grip my sweating glass, close my eyes and curse my father.

He's at the fourth stage when it's finally over. He's slurring and shaking and verbose. Skin beckons for the money and I chuck it across. He holds up my little pouch with the embroidered hearts and pours out the contents. They settle on the baize with a soft, grating sigh.

'Shee.. tol' you I haddit covered.'

I hadn't looked inside the bag. When Dad called, I had just followed his instructions and taken it from his drawer. They really are gold coins. They crouch in the middle of the table glinting and winking in the lamplight.

'What the fuck?' Skin is standing up. He speaks slowly, enunciating every word. 'Where the fuck did you get these?'

Dad hiccups out a laugh and slaps the air. 'Tol' you I could pay.'

One thing about Dad - he's always been a happy drunk.

'Where did you get them?' Skin's hands are knotted at his sides.

Dad's still semaphoring his humour. He grunts with laughter and points a shaking finger at me, 'Her. She got them.'

There's a shift in the air; in the cone of light above the table, the dust-motes tumble and crash.

Skin picks up a disc between thumb and finger and steps towards me. I can see the vein pulsing in his neck. 'Princess? Spun them out of thin air?'

Dad's eyes are half closed, his face seamed with fatigue. 'Yeah,' he slurs, 'that's it; she's magic, my daughter.'

The skin feels tight across my chest. I've been waiting for

something like this to happen since Mum died. I should have moved out months ago. Dad's slumped across the table, his hands splayed amongst the debris as if he's praying. It would make a good still life - scattered cards, empty whisky bottle, water jug still blistered with condensation, and the little pile of gold. 'Dad?' He's going bald. There's a pale circle of skin, like something newborn, on the back of his head. I've never noticed it before.

'Now here's the thing …' Skin's voice is soft and avuncular now, 'Those coins look very familiar. I need to have a little chat with your dad.' He clicks his fingers and the squat guy appears at my side. 'Take her outside.'

'You've got your money.' My breath's fast and jagged. 'Dad? Wake up.'

'Take her out.'

Skin's sidekick bundles me towards the door. I'm pulling away and slapping at him but it's like trying to fight a troll. Over his shoulder I can see Skin moving towards Dad with something heavy, metallic and two-handled.

'No!' My heart's rattling with the same clacking urgency as my spinning wheel. 'They're my coins. They're nothing to do with Dad.' I don't even intend to say it. The words spool out. 'I can get you more.'

Skin turns, the bolt-cutters dangling at his side.

'I just need a bit of time.'

We strike a deal: Skin keeps Dad. I go home. I have 24 hours to bring him the coins.

Big Ben's tolling midnight as I start up my little Fiat. I break all the speed limits getting out of Bermondsey. Maybe I'll be caught for running a red light. I imagine the comforting solidity of a British bobby. But the streets are empty. At home I waste precious minutes standing under a cold shower, washing off the touch and stench of the club. I lean my head against the glass, watching the water droplets snake and bump blunt-nosed down the screen.

If I contact the police, Dad's dead.

If I don't come up with more gold coins, he's dead.

If I don't tell Skin where they came from, he's dead.

I eye up the house phone. They've taken my mobile, but I could ring the police now. I pick up the receiver. I haven't used it for ages. It feels solid and reassuring against the skin of my palm. The ring tone is a comforting purr. I imagine trying to explain. Would they believe me? How long would it take them? How many men would they send? The club door squats at the foot of a narrow flight of stairs. No room to swing a battering ram. It's a massive, bolted thing, with a gridded hatch, and then there's a maze of corridors leading to the card room. It would take them hours to get in; seconds to kill Dad.

I search the house; his room first. I drag everything out of cupboards and wardrobes and drawers and side tables. I look under beds and on top of closets. I peer into the fridge and the freezer and the microwave and the oven and the washing machine. I dig in the coffee pot and the sugar jar and the flour canister. Nothing. When I go to the shed it's already getting light. The moon's still a faint, mother-of-pearl button, but in the east a line, like water on silk, is staining the sky luminous grey.

The shed's full of Dad's crap. Rusty tins of screws and nails, dried up pots of varnish, thick-skinned paint, empty cans of car oil; all furred with dust and cobwebs. He gave up DIY when Mum died. I pull it apart, breaking my nails and grazing my legs. Nothing. When I come crashing out into the light I see the squat bloke from the club. He's sitting on the garden bench shoving a McMuffin into his face. He nods his bald ogre head at me. I fist away my tears and stomp past him into the kitchen.

I drag the filing cabinet out from under the stairs. I don't even know what I'm looking for. Bank statements, mortgage stuff, receipts, birth certificates, utilities, old school reports. Nothing in the right section. Nothing unusual. Nothing that looks important. No sum of money Dad's forgotten. No share certificates. And then I see a thick, A4 cream envelope. My chest tightens. I yank it open and pull out the papers. I let out my breath and sit on the floor, clutching the envelope to my breast; Mum's will. She only left me two things. No trust funds. No gold jewellery. Nothing I can pawn.

I take the will into the kitchen and make myself a cup of tea. The sun's up properly now, barring the table with skewed parallelograms of light. Eight-thirty and it must be nearly 30 degrees. I phone in sick. It's bad timing; the fashion show is next month and the students will be desperate for my input. 'Tell them I'm sorry,' I say.

Mum left me her two most precious possessions: the spinning wheel and the sewing machine. I rest my face on my fingertips and stare at the paper. The words shift and swim, distorted as fish through ice. What was she thinking when she signed it? She would have still been fighting; she lived longer than they said. If she were here she'd know what to do. I close my eyes and listen to the birdsong and the faint shurring sound of the rush-hour traffic heading into the city. Inside there's the hum of the boiler and the creaking of settling boards. I know the sounds of this house; I've lived here all my life. Today the creaking seems louder than usual. It's probably just the wood contracting in the heat, but I fancy the house is groaning in sympathy with me. And then I hear it again, above my head. Mum's old sewing room. A footfall. One; then another, and a metallic clunk, which I recognise instantly. The spinning wheel handle. My heart contracts and I strain to listen. And then the room goes dark and I'm up on my feet, hands shaking, heart pounding.

'Oy!' It's the ogre bloke. His torso fills the window, blocking out the light. The bare dome of his head, angry as a boil, is dripping with sweat. He taps the glass with his phone. 'Skin says you've got until midnight. And no more phone calls.' He grins at me, his mouth wide, exposing teeth like a broken comb. 'We're watching you.'

Upstairs, the door to Mum's sewing room is ajar. It's my room now. I spin and sew while Dad stocks the recycling bin. I work with the same llama fleece that Mum used. Its fluffsome slipperiness makes the softest, lightest wool in the world. I push the door and breathe in the earthy, animal smell of llama. The sunlight spills into the landing, sharp and sweet as lemonade, and I blink against the brightness. Something shifts at the back of the room. My heart flutters. A silhouette detaches itself from the spinning wheel.

'Morning, Kate.' It's the lanky one in the sharp suit. He's standing straight now, shoulders back, relaxed. 'Found the money yet?'

'How did you get in?'

He picks up a skein of wool and rubs it between his fingertips. He has long, slim, tanned fingers. 'Where d'you get it from?'

I shrug and swallow, 'I don't know. Dad got it …'

'Not the money; the fleece. Who's your supplier?'

I grip the door jamb. 'Crowborough, down in Sussex.'

He lifts the skein to his face and inhales. His eyes are the same shade of caramel as the wool. 'You won't find the money.'

'I've got until midnight.'

He bowls the skein across to me. I fumble the catch and step into the room.

'It's nice stuff Kate, but it's not gold, is it?' He's moved closer. He stands over me as I pick up the wool.

I avoid his eyes. 'I'm wasting time talking.'

He places his hand on the small of my back and propels me towards the sewing machine. 'Sit down Kate. I've got a proposition for you.'

I don't like the way he keeps using my name. There's power in the knowledge of a name. When he steps away, I can still feel the echo of his fingers against my spine.

'How good are you? He slips off his jacket and drops it in my lap. 'Could you make something of this quality?'

The fabric spreads itself across the bare skin of my thighs. It still carries the heat of his body. I gather it up. Italian wool, lined with Bermberg rayon. When I rub it between my fingers, I can feel the stuff it's interlined with. The buttons are engraved with the designer's initials: RSS. Not someone I've come across.

'Italian, hand-stitched, basted fitting, interlined …' I look up at him and falter; his shirt is so finely woven, I can see the glow of his skin beneath the fabric. 'Yeah, I could make something like this; if I had a week, or a fortnight; and if I wasn't on a treasure hunt.'

'I want you to make this.' The muscles in his back shift beneath his shirt as he bends to open his sports bag.

'Make this and I'll get you your coins.' He drops a roll of paper at my feet.

I palm it out on my sewing table. 'It's a dress pattern.'

He claps his hands slowly. 'No shit.'

'What d'you want a dress for?'

'Can you make it or not?'

'I don't have time. I've got no fabric. And that corset will need bone.'

'You've got till midnight.'

'Impossible.'

He shrugs. 'Don't save your dad then.'

'I can't hand-stitch it in that time.'

'Use the machine. Sometimes you have to sacrifice craftsmanship on the altar of speed.'

He's taken a phrase I use for my students and distorted it. Don't sacrifice craftsmanship on the altar of innovation. That's what I tell my first-years.

'Sometimes we have to make sacrifices.' He empties the bag onto the floor. A mass of shimmering vermillion silk spills out.

'Start on that. I'll get the bone.' He plucks his jacket from my lap and walks out.

It's a stunning design. Simple but classy, with subtle contradictions. The bodice is boned and strapless. The fabric skims the hip then falls in a flared skirt. On one shoulder there's a ruched flounce with soft tulle roses. The front is demure while the back is slashed open to the waist in a deep vee.

I gather up my scissors, paper, pins, tape measure and chalk and get to work.

It takes me four hours just to cut the thing out. I'm becoming slow and clumsy. I prick my finger and the blood wells up in a fat ball and spills onto the fabric. At least it's red. I put my finger to my mouth.

'Have you eaten?'

I jump.

'D'you like sushi?'

I shrug. 'Have you got the coins?'

'Come and eat.'

'Is my dad okay?'

'I've got the bones; for the corset. You look tired. You need to eat something.'

I'm threading the machine when he comes back with a glass of water and a plate of sushi. I click on the new spool, pull the crimson cotton through the thread guides and onto the tension discs, thread it through the lever and finally through the eye of the needle. My fingers follow the route automatically, muscle-memory making them steady and sure. He's standing next to me, so close I can feel the heat from his body. For one moment I think he might feed me a piece of sushi. I imagine opening my mouth, the brush of his fingertips against my lips.

'I made them myself.' He lifts a tendril of my hair. 'First you skin and cure the fish, then you cut up the flesh and wrap each piece in a shiny seaweed skin.'

'I'll eat later.' I breathe slowly, line up the fabric, lower the foot and start the machine.

It takes me hours. Sometimes he leaves me alone and sometimes he sits in the paisley armchair, tapping on his Ipad. I used to sit there and watch Mum. When I'm ready to thread the ribs through the channels I've stitched into the bodice, he's at my side again. His fingers graze mine as he places the whalebone pieces next to the machine.

I finish it at half past ten. I click up the foot and cut the dress free. It's one of the most beautiful things I've ever made. The woman who's going to wear it must be very tall. I imagine a model: blonde, Amazonian.

'Its done.'

He takes it from me gently, cradling it across both arms.

'It's perfect.' He feeds a velvet hanger through the neck and hooks it on the door.

I roll my shoulders, ease out my aching back. 'Where's the money?'

'Drink this and I'll get it for you.' He hands me a glass. 'It's good for muscle fatigue.'

I inhale cinnamon and mint and down it in a few quick gulps.

I wake to darkness and the ringing of the doorbell. I stumble up, disorientated, feel my way to the light-switch. The dress and the man are gone. On the floor, next to the spinning wheel, is a pile of gold coins.

Skin and the ogre give up on the front door and come round the back. I hear them pounding through the kitchen and up the stairs. I'm still fingering the sleep from my eyes when they burst in. Skin's thoughts chase themselves across his pocked skin, and he finally smiles. 'Well, well, princess.

Looks like you've come up trumps for Daddy.'

'Where is he?'

'He's fine.' Skin holds up both hands and wiggles his fingers at me. 'All intact.'

'So let him go.'

He plonks himself down on the little paisley chair. 'Now, here's the thing, bit of a dilemma; your dad's story is that he won them in a poker game last week, up in Soho. Says he gave me the whole lot last night; that he doesn't have any more.' He steeples his fingers beneath his chin, his wedding ring glinting like a fat brass eyelet. 'But here you are with another tidy little pile. And Dave here says you haven't left the house.'

The silence balloons out between us. Skin breaks first. His eyes narrow and he leans back, crossing his ankles. 'Well princess, if you've got nothing to say, I guess we're back at the starting line.' He stands up. 'Same old, same old. Midnight tomorrow. Get me more or tell me where they came from.' He signals to the ogre to collect up the coins. 'Otherwise your dad and I are going to do more than talk.' He pats me on the head, 'And don't worry about being alone here all night - Dave'll keep an eye on you.'

When I'm sure they've gone I make myself a sandwich and climb into bed with my laptop. I look up Mr Skin. Know your enemy. I can't find much. Bermondsey born. Used to import furs and owned a tannery. He's now the registered owner of three London bars with gambling licences. Married a woman called Jemima Stilt twenty-five years ago. One son. I find that is Jemima living at an address in a smart street in Fulham. Perhaps they're divorced or separated. Nothing that will help me.

I wake up to the smell of bacon and the shrill peeping of pigeons. I find the suit-man in the kitchen.

'Sit down. What's the saying? Breakfast like a king?'

'I'm telling Skin it was you who got the money.'

He plates up bacon, eggs and tomatoes. 'He won't believe you.'

'He might.'

He pulls out a chair and gestures for me to sit down. Today he's wearing Diesel jeans and Converses and another white shirt. He sips his coffee and shoves his fingers through his hair. 'Can't be easy, living with your dad. Must get claustrophobic sometimes.' He slides his hand towards me. I watch his perfect flesh-levelled nails smoothing the grain of the wood.

'It's fine.'

'I can help you.' His hand edges nearer mine, his cuff sliding up to reveal a tanned wrist and a gold Patek Philippe watch. 'Make me another dress and I'll get the money. Same old, same old.'

This time it's a silver column frock. Italian double crepe with a boat neckline and a cowl at the back. Floor length again. Same measurements. Outside, Ogre sits and smokes in the shade by the pond. Inside, I sew and the suit watches. It's hotter than ever. The sun tracks its way around the room and I sweat and prickle in its sticky heat. I wonder how Dad's faring; whether he's drunk, or shaking and sweating in a hung-over haze.

At lunchtime, Suit-Man comes back with a prawn and avocado salad and a massive plug-in fan. It burrs and whirrs alongside the buzz of the sewing machine and the rustle of crepe. We don't speak, but I feel his eyes on me, and when he brings the food our hands touch, and something shivers down my spine and shifts in my groin. I ask what his name is and he just shakes his head.

When the dress is finished, my fingers are raw. The sewing table is scattered with tiny flakes of my skin. I drink his tea and fall asleep again. Same old, same old.

Skin and the ogre wake me at midnight. The dress is gone and, on the carpet, next to the spinning wheel, is another pile of gold.

'Now, here's the thing,' says Skin, 'the reason why I'm so touchy about the money is that it's mine.' He taps a coin thoughtfully against his teeth. 'I'm impressed with you, I really am. Good looking, poker face, I'll grant you that.' He flicks the disc into the air and it spins back into his waiting hand. 'These coins are from the same batch.'

'Is Dad all right?'

'I don't welch on a deal.' He holds the coin to his face and scowls. 'I recognise that smell.'

He's right; they do have a weird scent. It's some kind of perfume, heavy and sweet and feminine. I noticed it yesterday.

He tosses the coin back onto the pile. 'But none of my money's missing. So guess you're just the goose that lays the golden eggs.' He massages his earlobe. 'If you won't tell me where you got it, we're just going to have to do it all over again.'

The next morning the suit brings me croissants and a pain au raisin. He leans across the table and wipes a fleck of pastry from the corner of my mouth.

This time it's a ball dress in eau de nil water silk. Classic A-line with embroidered detail on the bodice and a deep vee back.

'Did she like the others?'

He smiles and sweeps back his shiny, floppy hair. 'Loved them.'

'She's very tall. Is she your girlfriend?'

'You look like your mother.' He points to the photos on the kitchen wall. There are dozens of monochrome shots of Mum and Dad. I'm in some of them as a baby and toddler. Dad put them up when Mum died.

'Must be unbearable sometimes.'

I shrug.

'Surrounded by this. Stepping into her shoes, her skin …
I bet you do everything she did: cooking, cleaning, sewing,
fetching your father …'

'We better get started.'

'Don't you want to escape? Slough it all off?'

I push away the plate. 'Let's get on with it.'

The back of this dress is as low as the first one. The vee is deep
enough to reveal the curved cheeks of the wearer's buttocks.
Skin would probably have girls working in his clubs. I see
tall, blonde, Eastern Europeans. Perhaps he traffics them.
Forces them to work. The Suit can probably take his pick.
I imagine him dancing with her, his hands sweeping down
to the base of her spine, smoothing the creamy swell of her
bottom.

'Your dad's okay.'

'What?'

'You look upset. He's okay. Trust me.'

We do it all over again. My fingers are raw. My skin is
scattered like shed scales over the sewing machine table.
Maybe third time lucky. This time I do one thing differently;
when I finish, I only pretend to drink his tea. I close my
eyes, lay my head on my arms and make my breathing deep
and even. I hear him leave and go outside. There's the slam
of a car door, footsteps on the stairs and then I can feel him
back in the room. There's the tinkle of metal, and the soft
rustling of fabric. I peer through my lashes. The money is
on the floor. It smells stronger than ever - sweet and warm,
with hints of rose and vanilla. He takes the dress from its
hanger, holds it in his arms, and stares at it. Perhaps he's
examining the stitching or the fabric. He drapes it over the
little paisley chair, and starts shedding his clothes.

He unbuttons his shirt. His fingers are neat and quick. He's slipping it off, and hanging it over the spinning wheel, then stepping out of his trousers. Beneath his honeyed skin he has the spare, tapered muscles of a long-distance runner. He picks up the dress and steps in, pulling the fabric up over his legs, his thighs, his flat stomach and up to his shoulders. He stands tall and straight in front of the mirror, twisting and turning and stroking the fabric.

I open my eyes and sit up. 'Good fit.'

He whirls around.

'Can I help you with the back?'

He stares at me, slack-faced, and then he nods. I straighten the shoulders, and tug up the bodice. He smells of sweat and spice. I turn him round to check the fit at the back.

'Sometimes,' he says, 'don't you want to step into someone else's skin?'

I place my lips on the golden down of his neck. When he doesn't move, I kiss his shoulder blades and run my tongue down the long, long length of his spine, to the dip between the swell of his buttocks. He's gasping and turning and cupping my face in his hands, and yanking at the dress, and my perfect seams are ripped apart, my hand stitched bodice with the whalebone ribs is torn in two. He's kicking it off and gathering me up and pulling me down to the floor on top of the silky folds of fabric. I kneel on top of him and pull off my t-shirt.

'I still don't know your name.'

He tacks his fingers around one of my nipples. 'If you know my name, you'll know my secret.'

'Tell me.'

He smiles and shakes his head and slides his hands under my hair, to the nape of my neck, and pulls me down. I put my lips on his and dissolve into him.

I wake up alone and naked in bed. The sun's up. I've missed

Skin's midnight visit. I ache all over. When I put my fingers between my legs I'm damp and sticky. Downstairs someone's in the kitchen. No smell of bacon; maybe croissants today. I want to call his name, but I don't know it. In the mirror my skin is puffy and stitched with rash-like trails from his stubble. I splash my face with water, run a brush through my hair, dab my lips with gloss, and pull on shorts and a shirt.

I stand in the hallway, listening to the clink of crockery and cutlery. My stomach's swirling and my heart's knocking at the base of my throat. I check my hair in the mirror, take a breath and walk in.

'Hi, princess.'

'Dad.'

He walks across to me, as stiff and slow as a spaceman. 'Don't look so shocked. I'm okay. I'm okay.'

When he hugs me, I inhale sweat and alcohol and smoke. 'Skin let you go?'

'He found out where the money came from.'

I push Dad away. 'How? Who told him? What's he going to do?' I'm shaking.

'God knows. All hell's going off down there. Skin announces that he knows where the money came from, and then his wife pitches up - ex-wife - and he chucks me out.' Dad hands me a mug of tea. 'It's good to be home. I was living on peanuts, Big Macs and Jack Daniels.' He takes a sip and points to the ceiling. 'What's been going on up there? I get home and you're dead to the world. I take a peek at the sewing room and it's full of those bloody coins.'

'They're still there?' I race upstairs. The perfume's even stronger now. The room is awash with golden liquid air. It shimmers on the ceiling like reflected water. The dress lies in a warm, glistening puddle on the floor.

'Been sewing, love?'

I gather it up and hold it against my face. It smells of nothing.

'The college called. Asking how you were. Something about that fashion show next month.'

'Dad, did you see the other man? The tall one.'

'Rum?'

'Who?'

'Rum. Early twenties. Tall, dark.'

'It was him. He gave me the money. I've got to help him. Skin will kill him.'

Dad shakes his head. 'Rum? He gave you the money?'

'I'm going round there.'

I shove on flip-flops and grab the car keys. Dad scratches his head, slow and hung-over.

As I run out he shouts after me. 'They won't let you in - he's gone mad on security. You'll need the password.'

The metal hatch slams shut.

'Hey!' I rap on the door and put my mouth so close to the barred square that I can taste the metal. 'Once upon a time!'

The door looks like it's been stopping undesirables for centuries. It was probably soundproof once, but now its warped and cracked. Through the gaps I can hear a muffled argument. The hatch thwacks open again and Dave the Ogre peers out.

'That was last week's code.'

'You know who I am. Let me in.'

Bolts screech and rattle, and the door grumbles open. I shove past him. My flip-flops slide on the tiles and I kick them off and carry on down the corridor, into the room where I found Dad three nights ago.

The carpet sucks at the soles of my feet. Skin has shuttered out the summer and everything's the same as before. It could be midnight; low lights, air thick with stale cigarettes and beer. Skin is sitting at the bar with a woman.

'What have you done with Rum?'

'Is this her?' The woman looks me up and down.

'She's Kate.'

'The one you've been seeing?'

'I told you,' he sighs, 'I wasn't seeing her. It was business.'

'You spent two nights at her house.'

'Jemima, Jemima.' Skin leans across to stroke the woman's face and she slaps him away.

She smiles at me lazily. 'We're always attracted to the bastards, aren't we?'

Skin holds up both hands. 'I've done nothing wrong, Jem.'

'Where's Rum?'

The woman, Jemima Stilt, Skin's wife, slides off the stool. As she comes closer the cloying sweetness of her perfume wraps itself around me. It's the same scent of the coins.

'What's my son to you, Miss Timotei?' She flicks a strand of my hair.

'Your son?'

Skin nods. 'Yeah; Rum - our son. We'd like to know where he is too. He's gone.'

Jemima's caramel eyes narrow and her pupils dilate as she stares at me. 'We'll find him. We're a close family, you know.' She crosses her fingers and holds them up to my face. 'We're tight. It was me who gave him the coins.' She touches my hair again. 'I always wanted a little girl. She'd have looked lovely in fur.' She shrugs. 'Who knows, maybe a grand-daughter?'

I swipe away the sweat pricking at the back of my neck and she blinks her gold-flecked eyes at me. 'Hot, isn't it? Did Skin tell you it used to be a tannery? This was the drying area. You can still smell the blood sometimes, seeping up from the boards.' She strokes her fur gilet. 'I used to get involved too. Skinning was my favourite. If you did it right it would be like peeling a stocking off a pointed foot. Leaving us already? Surely not.'

I try to forget him. The days slide into each other as I concentrate on keeping Dad sober. He stays home, shadowing me, close as cling-film. The house feels cramped and oppressive. Even my clothes feel tight. I cook and clean and prepare my students for the fashion show. The heat-wave lingers and I can't sleep at night. I toss and turn, and dream of him touching me, inside out with longing. Every morning I'm sick from lack of sleep.

The day of the show dawns hot and sultry. They say it's going to break tonight. South of the Thames it's soft and sunlit but, to the north, the sky's a purple bruise. I set up our stand at the Art Centre, hand it over to the students and go grab a coffee. There's a list of exhibitors on the counter. One name leaps out at me.

I find his stand in a corner at the back of the hall. He watches me approach, his caramel eyes laughing.

'You took your time.'

'Didn't know your name.'

'Worked it out now, though?'

'RSS. Your initials. Dad and Mum's surname. Stilt and Skin. You took them both.'

He points to the sign above his head.

RUMPLESTILTSKIN

'So,' he says, trailing a finger along the seam of my lips, 'I think we should work together. That's what Mum and Dad did. Her family were tailors; his were furriers.'

I should walk away.

As I step towards him, the lights flicker. From outside, there's the unmistakable rumble of thunder.

I won't tell him I'm pregnant yet, but I don't think he'll mind. Mum used to read me the fairytale. I can't recall the heroine's name, but I do know what Rumplestiltkskin always wanted: her firstborn child. In one version, the earth splits and swallows Rumplestiltskin up. When Rum kisses me and rubs his skin against mine, the ground shudders beneath my feet, but I hold on tight.

AUTHORS' BIOGRAPHIES

James Agombar
The Spectre of San Estradus

James Agombar lives and works in Essex, UK. This is his first published work. He is a member of Southend Poetry and Prose and also a student doing a degree in Humanities mixed with Art History. Having travelled through many countries spanning six continents, he takes inspiration from a wealth of culture and personal experience. His ideology bares resemblance to that of Pliny the Younger, in which he believes that creativity and human progress comes from leisure before it comes from working life. That is the excuse he uses anyway.

Montague Chambers
The Swedenborg Angle
(winner of round 2)

Montague started writing when he was at School, but even at an earlier age (8-9) he used to make up stories on family holidays, about the area they were staying in and the landscape.

He started working life as a professional archaeologist and spent nearly 30 years working around the country in Essex, Herefordshire and the north of England. His writing name of Montague Chambers was taken from an old warehouse, when he was excavating a Roman villa in London. He supervised the first modern excavation of the wall fabric on Hadrian's Wall since 1911 and later was Assistant Director of Archaeology on the Channel Tunnel development.

He attended University College, Durham, obtaining his BA in 1987 and in 1994, his PhD on the archaeology and architecture of Durham Castle.

He writes in his leisure time, and was the runner up in a Short Story competition at his workplace. This encouraged him to do more with his writing and he started sending it off to competitions. His short stories have been long and short listed in a number of competitions. He recently won Second Prize from the Scottish Federation of Writers' with his story "The Soldier" whilst his flash fiction story "In the Beginning" was awarded a Highly Commended in the same competition.

He now works at a UK university, as an officer, in the research school and lives on the edge of the North York Moors, with his cat Tiberia (aka Squeaky).

JOSEPH DEGAND
ORIN SLEW

Joseph Degand is a full-time marketeer and publicizer with a passion for writing fiction in his spare time. He lives in Lincoln, UK with his wife, Heather, but is originally from New Jersey, USA. This is his first published fictional piece; however, he has written several more short stories and a novella that he is excited about sharing with the world in the future. Joseph finds inspiration for his writing in a variety of ways, mostly by considering the "What Ifs" of everyday life.

KIRILL ILUKIN
CORPSE ON A GURNEY

Kirill Ilukin is a Russian freelance game writer. His passion for dark fantasy led him to enter the Luna Press contest and see his first short story being shortlisted.

ANTHONY LAKEN
HARIX

Anthony Laken has been creating fantasy worlds since he can remember. Writing has always been part of his life and he hopes it will remain that way.

Anthony has had a few jobs: working in a now defunct video store, cutting up boxes at night, and teaching, but would love to turn writing into his profession.

He lives in the grey twilight of South East London with his fiancé and son.

You can follow him on Twitter: @ajlaken

K.J. LYMER
WITH MY EVERY BREATH

K.J. Lymer is a designer and illustrator who decided to take the plunge into the deep, dark worlds of speculative fiction and has been keeping his head above water ever since. He lives in the port city of Southampton, not far away from the forgotten ruins of an ancient Roman fort where there was found a sacrificial altar dedicated to a mysterious pagan goddess. 'With my Every Breath' is his first foray into the dominions of steampunk and gaslight fantasy, but with a twist – its setting takes place on the other side of the pond in Toronto and not neo-Victorian London. It was also written to celebrate the 150th anniversary of the publication of Alice's Adventures in Wonderland. When not combing the landscape for rabbit holes into other realms, K.J. can be found pursuing imaginative endeavors on his micro-Babbage engine involving the processing of words and the illustrating of scenes from myth and legend.

Visit squeakingcat.wordpress.com for more details.

IAN MCCAWLEY
LE MAUVAIS PAS

Ian McCawley specialises in fantasy, horror and suspense short stories, and is also working on his first crime novel. He is a former journalist and his writing draws on his experiences working in the normally mundane but sometimes stranger-than-fiction world of local media.

He now plies his trade in PR, where he tries to imbue banal business writing with colour and wit. An example would be a recent comment piece for a client about data storage sprinkled with religious symbolism, Pink Floyd lyrics and a reference to wrestling villain Giant Haystacks. Ian's favourite authors include Mo Hayder and Stephen King.

ANNA MILON
SOVEREIGN

Anna is an undergraduate student of English Literature at Royal Holloway College, University of London. She is currently writing a dissertation on the works of Tolkien and Yeats and runs a Tolkien Society in her free time. Among various literary hobbies, Anna makes time for archery and historical re-enactment. Her current aspiration is to achieve a career in creative writing.

SALLY MITCHAM
SNOW WHITE

Sally has recently won a local non-fiction writing competition and currently blogs about life with her special needs child. She is working on a young adult fantasy novel.

SAM PAYTER
THE FINAL RECKONING
(WINNER OF ROUND 1)

Sam Payter lives in South Somerset with his wife and baby daughter. He has been interested in stories, especially fantasy, since his mum started reading The Hobbit to him as a young child. Next came Lord of the Rings, then David Eddings, Raymond E Feist and so on. He always wanted to write his own stories and so took the experience of writing his dissertation and applied the same process to writing a novel. The result was a disaster, but the seed had been sown. He started writing short stories, whilst simultaneously reworking his novel. He would love a career where someone pays him to sit and write stories all day.

BARBARA STEVENSON
WHERE THE OCEAN MEETS THE SKY

Barbara Stevenson is a veterinary surgeon and writer living with various animal companions in Orkney. She writes mainly short stories and sketches, with the odd silly poem thrown in. Some of her short stories have been published in anthologies and in 2014 she had a couple of sketches performed in the Tron theatre in Glasgow. Her first novel will be out in February 2016, with Yolk Publishing and she is currently working on a murder series set in Neolithic Orkney. As well as writing she enjoys walking, music and reading - preferably works which are a little off-centre.

You can follow Barbara on Twitter: @Boo2111 or on Facebook as Babs Stevenson.

SIMON WALPOLE
(WINNING ILLUSTRATION)

Simon Walpole is a freelance artist who specialises in Fantasy, SF, Horror and Ancient Warfare. His work is primarily hand drawn and done in inks and watercolours.

These can be seen in the recent Ancient warfare magazine, the first journal of the British Fantasy Society, as well as some upcoming historical novels.
OfficialWebsite:
   http://swalpole6.wix.com/handdrawnheroes

MELANIE WHIPMAN
ANOTHER SKIN

Melanie Whipman is a PhD student and an Associate Lecturer at the University of Chichester. Her prose and poetry has been broadcast on Radio 4 and published in numerous anthologies and magazines. Her debut short story collection, Llama Sutra, is due out with Ink Tears Press later this year. You can find her at www.melaniewhipman.com